LOVE IN BRUTAL DEVOTION

THE BRUTAL DUET BOOK 2

B J ALPHA

BJ ALPHA

Published by BJ Alpha

Edited by Cheyenne - Frogg Spa Editing

Proofread and edited by Dee Houpt

Cover Design by Haya In Designs

 Created with Vellum

LOVE IN BRUTAL DEVOTION

BJ ALPHA

AUTHOR'S NOTE

WARNING: This book contains triggers. It has sensitive and explicit storylines. Such as:

Violence

Graphic sexual scenes

Stalker tendencies

Birth control manipulation

Dub-con

Strong language

Scenes of past traumas.

It is recommended for readers ages eighteen and over.

DEDICATION

*To all my readers, who love reading smut as much as I do
writing it.
You're so dirty, you're going to need cleansing after this one.*

STOP!!!

This is smut on the highest level!

Is there a storyline? Meh. I think so...Consider the following before continuing...

Do you like:

Praise Kink?

Daddy Kink?

Dub-con?

Jealous/Possessive Men?

Breeding Kink?

Lactation?

Stalker?

BDSM?

Knife Play?

If you got excited reading the list, then you're in the right place. You can turn the page.

Enjoy!

PROLOGUE

Previously...

Rage

The anxiety bouncing off Lucas as the elevator travels up toward our penthouse apartment is unmistakable, and I can't help but feel guilty that I helped create that for him. Cole can sense it too; his eyes are filled with pity, and they keep drifting toward him followed by a childish glare in my direction, letting me know I caused this whole fucked-up situation.

I refuse to acknowledge the fact, instead resting lazily against the wall until the elevator comes to a stop. I push off and head toward the door.

"Cole. Cole, I . . ." Lucas attempts to speak to Cole, but his words are lost, and he doesn't manage to formulate a sentence. His face is ghastly pale, making me for the first time think there's more to his behavior than meets the eye.

Cole grips Lucas by the neck, pulling him in so his

forehead rests against his. It doesn't look like a lover's embrace, so I watch on.

"It's okay, brother. We got this." Cole grins, but Lucas shakes his head, refusing to listen.

I choose to ignore their little tiff and open the apartment door. The first thing to fill my nostrils is something of nostalgia, but I can't quite place what it is—something Italian smelling—making regret hang heavily in my stomach when I realize the effort my brothers have gone to for my homecoming. They know Italian food is my favorite.

Cole pushes past me. "Rage, this is Tia. Our Tia."

I turn toward him, and my eyes instantly clash with those so familiar to me, my heart feels like it's being ripped from my chest. I can't breathe, and my mind floats somewhere so high I can't reach it. My legs weaken as my chest tightens, air sucked so forcefully from my lungs, I lose all power and drop to my knees on a deafening wail.

It takes me so long to realize it's not my wail. Not my voice. It's hers.

The same one I drove away from five years ago. The same voice that ripped out my heart and shredded it to pieces, leaving it so mangled, not another living soul could get close enough again.

"Lucas? Lucas, what the hell's happening?" Cole is crying above her, but I can't move. My head is dropped to the ground, and my fists are balled tight as I kneel on the floor, shutting out everything around me.

This can't be real. This can't be her.

With them?

My head suddenly snaps up at the realization.

She's with them.

Rage fills my body, anger like nothing before. I see red, red so fucking deep there's never going to be enough blood to drain from their bodies.

I fly toward Cole. He's cradling her in his arms. He's cradling what's mine.

Mine!

Lucas tackles me to the ground; he's so quick, I forgot he was even here.

"Take her to the spare room. Now!" he screams toward Cole, who rushes away with my girl.

I hit his jaw with a satisfying crack, then throw my head back and slam it against his nose. I ignore his words and his grunts of pain when I hammer my fist into his chest.

I want her back. I need her fucking back here with me where she belongs.

Mine.

I wrap my legs around his body and use them to throw him off me, quickly jumping to my feet. I rush toward the corridor, but Cole stands there, his eyes mirroring mine, fierce with rage.

I spit blood from my mouth.

"What the fuck are you doing, Rage?" He glares at me like I'm a psychopath, his eyebrows furrowing in confusion.

"He doesn't know, Rage. He doesn't know." I can

sense Lucas standing behind me, but his words do little to relax me.

"Get the fuck away from the door!"

Cole ignores me. Instead, he looks over my shoulder at Lucas, asking, "Doesn't know what?"

"I said. Get. The. Fuck. Away. From. The. Door." My voice gets deadlier on each word.

"Doesn't know fucking what?" Cole's unraveling. Even I can sense it in my state.

"It's her." Lucas's words sound broken even to my unapologetic ears. I refuse to listen to anything other than the whimpers behind the door.

"Her?"

My fists ball tighter, the blood from my knuckles dripping to the floor.

"Tia."

My head spins back in Lucas's direction. "That's not her fucking name!"

He licks his cracked lip. "It's her name now, brother."

The tight band around my last bit of self-control snaps, and I lunge for him once again, slamming him up against the wall with such force the plaster cracks.

Cole's arm tightens around my neck in a choke hold, but I refuse to give in. I refuse to release the bastard who betrayed me.

"Enough, Rage. Enough!" Cole tugs me back harder, but I let my fingers grip Lucas's neck tighter. I'm acutely aware that he isn't fighting, almost accepting his fate.

His lips begin to turn blue, but my mind is so

contorted in rage, I refuse to acknowledge anything other than the red haze surrounding me.

I hate him so much.

"Her name's Thalia. She's mine." I whimper lowly as realization dawns on Cole's devastated face.

I hate them all.

CHAPTER
ONE

T ia

I clutch at my chest; it hurts so bad. I've only ever felt like this once before, the first time I lost him. I thought I'd never recover. I guess in a way, I never have.

Their voices bounce off the walls, and I close my eyes, willing this all to be a dream. A sick, fucked-up dream.

I can still feel Cole's arm band around me protectively as he stepped us forward to proudly introduce me to his brother.

And then, my eyes locked with his and my world came crashing down around me.

Jace.

He recognized me instantly, and the same heartache mirrored mine as my body crumbled and Cole caught me, cradling me to his chest while all hell was breaking loose around me.

A harsh slam in the corridor makes my stomach drop

as I suck in a frightened breath. I edge off the bed. My feet find the carpet on trembly legs, unsure what to do.

A scuffle and a plea from Cole makes me rush toward the door. Swinging it open without thought, I take in the scene before me.

Cole has Jace in a chokehold, but Jace doesn't relent on his determination to strangle Lucas, who's standing still, almost like he's resigned himself to death. Panic floods my veins when I see Lucas's blue lips.

I spring into action, charging forward. "Please, Jace." My voice is a gentle plea as I touch Jace's hand, and the connection is immediate. There's a zap between us, severing the hold on Lucas in an instant.

Jace takes a step back from Lucas, who gasps for air, then he turns his head toward me.

Blackness consumes his eyes, and I stare into his orbs, entranced by the darkness now consuming him. Hate and hurt mar his features, making my heart stutter.

My eyes slowly rake over his body from top to toe, like we're the only two people in the room.

His boots are unlaced, his jeans fit him well, and he wears a leather jacket with a tight black T-shirt beneath it. Tattoos creep out over the T-shirt and up his neck, framing his face.

His balled fists—also fully tattooed—shake precariously by his sides. My breath hitches when I see the anguish on his face, the rage now coated with hurt.

My lips move, but, in all honesty, I don't know what to say. "Jace, I—"

My words snap him out of the trance he was

standing in. Moving toward me, his arm snaps out and drags me back toward the bedroom.

I'm briefly aware of Cole and Lucas arguing as Jace shoves me back into the spare room, flinging me on the bed so hard, I bounce. The door slams shut behind him, and he looms over me with the same darkness in his eyes that I know all too well when he sees red.

"What the fuck are you doing here, Thalia?"

I swallow deeply, gathering my words. "I'm with Cole and Lucas." The tremble in my voice is evident, and I want to quash it. It makes me sound weak, and I hate it. I'm anything but weak. Not anymore.

He sneers at me in disgust. "With. Cole. And. Lucas." Each word he cruelly punctuates, each word sounding deadlier than the last.

His eyes roam over my body, from my naked legs up to my denim jean shorts and thin camisole. My nipples pebble under his scrutiny, making me thankful I'm wearing a bra. Then, they latch on to my necklace, the one holding the key he gave me five years ago.

His chest heaves up and down, and his Adam's apple bobs. "You kept it."

My fingers find the key, toying with it for comfort as always.

"You kept it," he repeats to himself.

My tongue darts out over my lips, and he watches the motion, his eyes transforming from disgust to lust in the blink of an eye.

He painstakingly slowly peels his leather jacket from

3

his torso, letting it drop to the floor with a thud. I stare at him in disbelief.

Jace didn't have a single mark on his body when he left me that morning, only the ones on his knuckles, the ones from his rage.

And now, this man standing before me, is covered in them.

He rushes me, flipping me onto my stomach while he fumbles to unbutton my shorts beneath me.

"Jace. What are you doing?"

He ignores my question even though it's obvious. "Tell me you don't want my cock, Thalia." His words drip with need, making my body vibrate with pleasure. His hand grips the back of my neck, holding me against the mattress as he tears my shorts and panties from my body.

I'm numb. Numb to his words, to his action.

His thick cock prods at my entrance before surging forward again and again. I lie still, unable to comprehend that it's my Jace fucking me like this. Like an animal.

"You're fucking mine, Thalia. Mine!"

The mattress squeaks with his movement, and I cringe when my pussy responds to his words, squeezing him in tighter as though determined to keep him inside me, while my mind is screaming to stop. My body betraying me.

"Acting like a fucking whore. Did they pay you for this pussy?"

I try to shake my head, but the hold he has on me won't allow me to.

"Do you let them cum inside you, Thalia?" I squeeze my eyes closed. "Fucking answer me!" He rams harder.

"Yes."

My pussy clenches around him and I release a whimper of need. "Please."

"Fuck!" He slams into me so hard it hurts, and a whimper drops from my lips. "I fucking hate you!"

Slam.

"Hate you so goddamn much, it hurts."

Slam.

My pussy flutters, and I wish it would stop. I should not be turned on right now, not with the vitriol leaving his mouth. But I can't help it. I want him. I want this.

"Fucking whore. Mine!"

He pulsates inside me, the grip on my neck and hip tightening as his cum floods my pussy.

His heavy breathing stops and he quickly withdraws, making my body shudder with both the empty chill and the loneliness suddenly consuming me.

Just like before.

I turn to find Jace sitting on the edge of the bed with his head in his hands. "I'm sorry," he mumbles the words at me but refuses to face me. I shuffle toward him, but he gets up and heads toward the door.

Leaving me to feel used and abandoned yet again.

CHAPTER
TWO

Cole

"Let them speak. Please." Lucas holds me back as Rage disappears in the room with Tia.

I spin to face him, and betrayal bubbles in my veins. "You knew?"

Lucas stares at me without a hint of remorse on his face. "Yes."

My head drops forward, and I close my eyes. "Jesus, Lucas. How could you?"

A chair scrapes across the floor, and I open my eyes to him sitting, watching me closely. "When I first saw her, I knew I had to have her." His voice comes out weak.

"She wasn't yours to fucking have!" I can't help but scream at him. He's acting so cool and collected, like he hasn't just ripped our lives apart. Like we haven't all just betrayed one another.

"She wasn't yours either." He stares at me. But his

words hit me hard, making me suck in air. He's right, she wasn't mine either.

"She is now!" I grind my teeth in temper. There's no fucking way I'll allow anyone to take her from me. Never.

The bedroom door opens, and I turn to face Rage. His eyes aren't as wild anymore, but now they appear broken, hurt. His jeans are open at the waist, and a sliver of panic hits me in the gut.

"What the fuck did you do?"

He smirks in my direction but refuses to acknowledge my words. Instead, choosing to ignore me, he moves toward the refrigerator.

I rush to the bedroom, and relief flows through me when I see Tia sitting up in bed in one piece. She hugs the sheets like a barrier.

"Are you okay, beauty?"

She shakes her head from side to side.

"Did he hurt you?"

Please say no.

"Not in the way you think." Her voice is delicate and broken, and, not for the first time, I want to kill Lucas for the situation he's put us all in.

"Did you know?" Her eyes latch on to me, begging me for the truth, so I stare straight back at her with confidence behind my words.

"Of course not."

She blows out a breath of relief. "Can you hold me?" Her voice trembles, and I spring into action, grateful that she still wants me, needs me as much as I need her.

I kick off my jeans and T-shirt, pull back the sheets,

and pull her toward me so she can rest her head on my chest while I stroke her hair.

I clear my throat, needing reassurance. "Did he . . . did he force you or anything?"

She chokes through a sob. "No."

I take hold of her jaw and tilt her head up to face me. I need her to know I'm not mad at her. "It's okay, Tia."

She shakes her head from side to side. "No, it's not, Cole. We . . ."

I stare at her; how can she not see I don't care what they did as long as she doesn't leave me? "I love you," I tell her, my heart hammering in my chest, longing for a response from her.

She licks her lips as though gathering courage. "We had sex. We had sex, and I didn't tell him to stop." She tears her eyes away from mine, blinking away unshed tears before bringing them back to me. "I'm sorry." My muscles coil on her words, and my pulse echoes in my ears, please say it. Please say it back. Tell me I haven't lost you to him.

"I love you, Cole."

My lips crash against hers in gratitude. In love and protection.

In clear devotion.

She's mine.

She might be his too, but she's ours.

RAGE

Lucas gives me his back. The coward turns and walks toward his office, but I refuse to let him get away from me so easily.

I deserve answers.

I slam the door behind us, but he doesn't so much as flinch, not even knowing he's cornered in a room with a man they call "Rage" for good reason.

Instead, Lucas bends and unlocks a drawer beside his desk. He pulls out a file and dumps it on his desk with a thud, then slumps back in his desk chair.

"It's all in there." He throws his arm out toward the file, and my feet move in its direction, unsure what he's insinuating.

Lucas sighs with defeat, his swollen eyes trained on the folder. The air is thick and heavy, and I know whatever sits in that folder, I'm not going to like. My heart thuds as I open the front page. It skips a beat when I stare at the photo of Thalia smiling back at me. Her blue eyes glowing and lighting up her face, she appears completely happy. While I've been living in perpetual misery, she's been happy.

Hate bubbles inside me once again.

My hand shakes as I turn the page listing her details. I take the sheet in my hand as I scan over the fact she works behind a bar, the very same bar that Lucas sent Cole to only a couple of months ago.

I snap my eyes over to him accusingly. "You sent him there? You knew and sent him there?" Betrayal like no other turns my stomach. My own brother set this up. He orchestrated the whole damn thing.

"I did." He chokes the words out, his voice thick with emotion.

My body trembles as his actions sink into my mind and deep into the pit of my stomach. My glare burns into him. "Tell me."

Lucas stares at me blankly.

"Tell me everything!" I drop the sheet and stab my finger on the folder. "Tell me when this fucking started!"

He swallows hard and his lip cracks a little more as he opens his mouth to talk. "Six months ago, I got a lead."

I suck in a sharp breath, and my legs threaten to give way, so I steady myself with my hands on the desk. My head drops forward. Six fucking months?

He knew her location for six months and never told me. I squeeze my eyes shut to stop the sting in them, but it doesn't stop my heart constricting with a pain I recognize all too well when it comes to her.

"I . . ." He brushes his hand over his head. "I took a visit there. To make sure it was her."

I breathe in a large gulp of air, knowing he chose to go and see her without me.

"I sat in the bar and watched her. She was so fucking beautiful, but she didn't even know it. There were guys flocking round her, but she refused to acknowledge any of them." My hands tighten on the desk, knowing about all the men watching her. What's mine.

"I knew then she was loyal."

I scoff at his words. "Loyal?" There's not a loyal bone in her fucking body, not anymore.

"I wanted to talk to her." Lucas laughs to himself, but there's no humor behind his voice. "I even came close once. I'm twenty-five years old, and the first time I'm attracted to an actual woman, I can't even speak to her."

I choose to ignore the pity I feel toward him.

"I followed her home."

I snap my head up and spin to face him because did he just say he followed her home?

Lucas stares down at the table as though embarrassed by his admission. "I just wanted to make sure she got home okay." When he raises his head toward me, I can see the truth written all over his face. I grind my jaw at the thought of him keeping this from me. "I knew the moment I told you, you'd go rushing in and take her from me. From us."

My chest puffs out in anger. "Because she's fucking mine!"

He shakes his head. "I hope that's not true, brother."

He licks his cracked lip. "Because if that's true, then you just ripped our hearts out. You just ruined our family. We love her, Jace, and she loves us too."

His words penetrate my soul. They slice through my already tattered heart and threaten to completely destroy me.

Because if that's true, where does that leave me?

LUCAS

Rage storms from my office and slams the door behind him. I gather up the file he left behind and unlock my drawer. I stare down at the remaining files in there with hate in my veins but also determination. A determination to protect those I love most in this world, even if it means hiding the truth.

Carefully, I place the file over the top of the others, lock the drawer, and open my laptop. Casting aside my anxieties of potentially losing Tia, I concentrate on my task at hand.

The months I spent watching over Tia at night while she slept were some of my most pleasurable ones. I learned a lot in that time.

I need to dig deeper into Tia's past. To rid her of her nightmares, I'll find everyone in them.

All of them.

THREE

Tia

My feet hit the carpet, and I wince at the tender ache in my body left from last night. I relieve myself in the bathroom, wash my face, and make my way out into the living area, while Cole remains sleeping in bed.

I come to a complete stop when I see Jace on the couch staring in my direction, a darkness in his eyes far beyond anything I've witnessed before now. My stomach flips at the thought of how much he's changed, how much he now hates me.

We're both frozen, staring at one another, eyeing each other.

I take in how broad his shoulders are now, how he's become a man and I've missed the transformation. Pain lances in my chest, and I place the palm of my hand over it. He doesn't miss my action. His eyes narrow before his temple pulsates and his jaw locks tight. I swear I hear his teeth grind.

The atmosphere is so intense I suck in a sharp breath to try and regulate my erratic breathing. He wears a tight black T-shirt that stretches over his chest, tattoos run over his balled fists, up his arms, and snake out, covering his neck. My fingers itch to trail over them, explore each and every one of them.

My lips part to speak, but my mouth comes up empty.

Something snaps inside him, and he pounces over the couch with ease, his feet toe to toe with my own before I can blink.

Jace grips my neck and walks me backward until my back hits the wall. His nostrils flare as his eyes roam down my body, and I suddenly realize he's taken in the fact I'm wearing Cole's white T-shirt minus my bra. His fingers press harder on my neck, causing my eyes to bulge in panic.

"Did you fuck him?"

I stare up into his black eyes; they're so dark, I can't see his pupils, and hate oozes from them, causing me to shudder against him.

I slowly drag my tongue over my lips, wetting them. "No."

"You're going to finish it."

I narrow my eyes in confusion.

"You belong to me, Thalia. You're going to finish it with them." He spits the words, venom dripping from each word.

My heart hammers wildly in my chest and tears brim my eyes, clouding my vision. My lip trembles as I find my voice and say, "I won't."

He pushes me harder against the wall, so hard I feel every ridge of his solid body, every coiled muscle. Even his cock is rock hard and pressed flush against me.

My head hits the wall with a deep thud. "You will."

I shake my head. "I love them." My voice wobbles at my confession, and I cannot miss the jolt of his body when I say the words, nor can I ignore the pained expression that appears on his face.

He loosens his grip, his forehead meeting mine. "I hate you," he whispers against me, forcing me to close my eyes at the pain his words cause me.

I raise my hand to touch his face, but he backs away from me, as though burned, before spinning on his heel and heading toward the glass coffee table. I watch in horror as he picks it up and throws it against the wall with a roar. The table shatters, and both the bedroom and office doors fly open with Cole and Lucas racing into the living area in panic.

Jace spins to face us. His face is red, and the veins in his neck protrude. His eyes are frantic and wild, and I realize the man I'm staring at is no longer the Jace I knew.

He's Rage.

"Tia, go to our room." Cole moves to stand in front of me.

My body trembles, but I make no move.

"Tia. I told you to go to our room," he snaps at me.

I jump at his tone and rush off into the bedroom. Slamming the door behind me, I crumble to the floor.

Realizing that in choosing them.

I've lost him.

I finally have him back, and now I've lost him.

RAGE

I kick the punching bag again, harder this time.

My mind races with hate. How could she do this? How could she betray me like this? And choose them over me?

I imagine her with them. In our fucking apartment. Screwing them. Does she do them both at the same time? Has she turned into that much of a whore, she needs two cocks instead of one?

My body buzzes with hatred, desperate to inflict pain on someone, anyone—even myself.

I punch the bag harder this time, a roar coming from deep within me.

After all this fucking time, I finally have her, and she doesn't want me?

I punch the bag again, sweat dripping from my body and my knuckles cracking with the force of the impact. But I don't feel an ounce of pain. Only rage.

Maybe I just don't give her a choice? Force her to be

with me. Maybe she needs reminding how good we can be together.

I chug the water from my bottle and toss it into my bag.

It's time Thalia knows the man I've become. The monster she's made me.

He's filled with rage and hate.

He's brutal.

Brutally devoted.

TIA

After the door to the apartment slammed, Cole came in search for me and reassured me Jace just needed time to calm down.

He ran me a bath and told me the living room would be cleaned when I got out. He wasn't happy that he had to go to work for the night and peppered me with loving kisses that eventually made me giggle and shove his head away playfully. I love how broad and muscular he is, but with me, he's just a teddy bear.

He whispered that he loved me, and his shoulders dropped in relief when I whispered the words back to him.

There's no way I could ever leave him. Not now, not ever.

Jace Matthews broke my heart, but it was Cole Maguire who fixed it.

And Lucas? Lucas became the glue that holds us together.

I'm just not sure how I can make this work with them when I still ache to feel him.

Long for him.

Love him.

Dragging the comb through my hair one final time, I place it on the dresser and stare at the girl reflected in the mirror.

There was a time in my life when I couldn't stand to look at her, hated her even. She was weak and vulnerable, defeated and broken. She was a young girl with no hope.

But not anymore.

Now, staring back at me is a woman with fire in her eyes and strength in her veins. She's been to hell and back, and she's still standing. I refuse to be the weak girl I once was. I refuse to be controlled by anyone, even Jace.

I need answers, and in order to get them, I need to speak to Lucas.

Stepping into the corridor, I make my way toward his office, and without knocking, I swing open the door and step inside.

His eyes fix on mine, and his Adam's apple bobs with trepidation.

I cross my arms over my chest, and his gaze goes to my breasts, causing my nipples to involuntarily pucker at his perusal.

I'm not sure Lucas even realizes he's eye fucking me, or if he just doesn't care that he's so blatant.

"Are you even sorry?"

He sighs, leaning back into his chair and dropping his pen on the desk. "No."

My eyebrows shoot up in shock, his words causing me to gasp. "No?"

Lucas leans forward. "No. You know why?" I shake my head and wait for him to speak. "Because if I hadn't done what I did—" He swallows hard. "I'd have never found you. Had you. Tasted you. Loved you."

My heart skips a beat, and my voice wobbles. "Did you set this up? Did you know Cole found me?"

He smiles like a Cheshire cat. "I was counting on it."

My heart jumps at just how cunning he is, how he orchestrated the whole thing to, what, bring us together?

"B . . . but you couldn't have known he'd want me." His intense eyes drill into my body, making me shudder. I fidget uncomfortably under his scrutiny.

"I know my brother better than he knows himself. I know everything there is to know about him. The way he was missing something, someone. And I knew from the first moment I saw you that you were his. Ours."

"And what about Jace? Where does he fit into all of this?"

He sinks back into his chair, slowly licking his lips with calculation. "That's on him."

"That's on him?" I repeat his words, and he nods at me.

"He's our brother." His voice is low and deliberate, as

25

though making a point, one that pierces into me with such sharpness I could mistake it for his knife. "I can share."

I choke on air. "You? Share?" My tone is condescending, even to my ears.

Lucas stares at me, his face a blank expression, but I don't miss the pain in his eyes. "It doesn't have to be with us," he snaps out.

"Us?" I raise an eyebrow in question, forcing his jaw to twitch. Because whether he meant to or not, he just included Cole.

He averts his gaze for the first time since I entered his office, and I know I've unnerved him.

"It's okay to want him too," I whisper into the room.

Lucas's eyes close on a tortured expression, as though it pains him to even accept the fact he wants Cole like that.

Suddenly, the very reason I even entered the office is forgotten because all I want to do is to take the hurt away from him. To reassure him.

I take a step toward him. And another.

His hand snaps out and he pulls me by the legs toward him, almost making me stumble into him.

I stare down into his eyes, and emotion wells in them. "Tell me I haven't lost you."

My heart constricts as his hands tighten on my thighs, holding me in place, willing me to cooperate.

"Tell me!" he demands.

I stare down into his determined gray eyes, not missing the hint of vulnerability in them, the longing.

LOVE IN BRUTAL DEVOTION

"You haven't lost me." My voice is so low I can barely hear it myself, but when he drops his forehead to my stomach and places a gentle kiss there, I know he heard me.

A single tear falls down my face as I hold his head against me. "I love you, Lucas."

His gaze snaps up to mine, and possession reflects in his eyes. "Say it again."

I choke the words out on a silent sob, "I love you."

He pushes back on his chair, putting distance between us. He pulls his knife from his pocket, and my face heats from thoughts of his intentions.

Lucas pulls the knife down the center of my dress. The tearing of it slices through the room, leaving the fabric pooling at my feet and me standing in only a small G-string. He sucks in a sharp breath, and his lips part. This man, this Adonis of a man, is so beautiful he makes my heart ache for his touch.

His eyes flare as he takes me in before unbuckling his belt with shaky hands. "Give me your hands, baby girl."

I hold out my hands for him, and he ties the belt around my wrists so tight it pinches into my skin.

Gently, he tucks my hair behind my ears, and I shiver under his tenderness before the blade of his knife cuts my panties from me, allowing them to drop to my feet.

"I thought I would lose you." He peers down on me from under his thick eyelashes. "I refuse to lose you."

I nod at his words.

"Tell Daddy you understand."

A flood of arousal hits me, and my cheeks flush with need. "I understand, Daddy."

He softly strokes my cheek with his fingers, causing a tremor of need to rack through my body. "Good girl. Now, scoot up on the desk and let Daddy show you how much he needs you."

My pulse quickens, and I do as he asks, scooting my ass up onto the desk while Lucas drops to his knees in front of me. He pushes my thighs farther apart, the grip on them tightening as he stares at my pussy, which is no doubt glistening with arousal.

"Daddy's little girl needs licking, doesn't she?"

My voice trembles with need, "Yes."

A languorous stroke of his tongue runs through my folds, making me whimper in response before he repeats the action.

"Mmm." He moans into my pussy, making me raise my ass off the desk with the vibrations.

The scruff on his jaw scrapes my legs as he grinds his face into me. Lucas pulls back slightly before blowing on my clit, and I want to drag his face back to my center, push him into me, and fuck his tongue.

"Please, Lucas."

His eyes—ebbing in anger—snap up to mine, and I instantly know I've overstepped. My heart hammers. His tongue flicks out over his wet lip, and his jaw sharpens.

Lucas stands, and I take in his clothed body against my naked one. I itch to tear off his shirt, for him to drop his pants and release his solid cock.

He flicks open his knife, startling me, and with one

hand on my chest, he pushes me so I'm flat against the desk. He slowly trails the tip of his knife down my body, down my stomach to my pussy, where he pauses. "I want to fuck your cunt with my knife, baby girl."

His voice is dark and coated in danger, but the sick part of me, the part of me that has lived on danger and in darkness for years, that part of me revels in this. Accepts this.

"Please, Daddy."

He spears me with the handle of his knife, and I arch my back into it.

"Such a pretty dripping cunt, fucking my knife." His hooded eyes stare down at my opening. The slick sounds of my body accepting his knife, accepting him, only turns me on further. An orgasm is racing toward me, and when he presses his fingers against my clit, I erupt around the smooth handle of his knife. I throw my head back and scream out my release, raising my head in time to see Lucas shoving his hard cock into my pussy. He slams into me over and over, making me clench around him.

"Daddy's cock is so hard for you, baby girl."

"Please. More."

"You're going to make Daddy come inside your pretty little pussy."

I squeeze around him, sending an expression of pleasure over his chiseled face as he pants out, "Fuck."

My tied hands grip onto my breast, and I offer it to him, knowing how much he enjoys sucking on my nipples.

He watches the motion with heavy eyes while he

pumps his hips over and over before he ducks his head to my breast. He begins sucking and nipping over the flesh before he finally sucks my nipple to the point of pain. I hold his head in place, loving the sensation of the pain with the pleasure, embracing it.

"Oh god, Lucas!"

"Fuck, you feel amazing, sucking my cock in your tight little pussy like a good girl."

My walls convulse, and a shudder takes over. Lucas lets me know he feels it too. He straightens, and his hooded eyes stare into mine before he tilts his head sideways and spits at my breast. I immediately rub in his spit over my nipple. The wetness soothes the sting left behind.

"Fuck. Fuck." He pulls out and slams in harder, causing my body to tense as his body stills. "Fuck." His lips part as he stares at me through his lashes. "Mine!" His cock pulsates deep inside me.

"Fuck, Daddy!" I scream into the room, my body tight in ecstasy as my pussy clenches around him, locking him in.

"Mine," I pant into the room, repeating his words.

Lucas belongs to me.

Me and Cole.

I'm just not sure where that leaves Jace, and with that awareness, a chill takes over my body, all the way to my core.

CHAPTER
FOUR

T ia

I spent the afternoon working on the illustrations I'm going to present as part of my coursework in the hope of winning a placement for a children's publishing house sponsored by the college I study at.

In the evening, I make pasta, and Lucas joins me at the dining table. We eat in a comfortable silence. Every once in a while, I feel his eyes on me, and I lift my head to find him watching me, only for him to gift me with a rare, soft smile.

Lucas offers to wash the dishes while I go shower.

As I tilt my head backward under the heat of the water, I comb my fingers through my hair, vaguely aware of the shower door opening. I relax in the knowledge that Cole is home earlier than expected. I smile to myself when I feel his presence behind me.

The hands that tweak my nipples feel different, not

31

as gentle, not as big. My spine jolts with awareness. This isn't Cole.

I can smell alcohol on his breath as he breathes in my scent. "Wassnn't expecting me, wasss you, baby?"

Jace is drunk. I can sense it in the slur of his words, the roughness of his touch when he palms my pussy and pushes his fingers inside. "Mmm, still tight. Did taking two cocks not stretch you?"

I whimper at his words, both turned on and disgusted.

Jace pushes my head down, angling my body so it's at a slight bend before removing his fingers and replacing it with the head of his cock. "This pussy belongs to me, Thalia." He surges forward, making me wince at being unprepared.

The aggression rolling off him comes through as he hammers into me from behind. One hand grabs a fistful of my hair and tugs it back, forcing my neck to stretch, and his eyes roam over my body from above. He drives into me, and the angle is so awkward, I have to stand on my tiptoes.

"Fuck, you're so damn beautiful." My pulse races at his admittance. "So beautiful." He pumps into me over and over. "Fuck! I'm gonna come." I expect him to pull out, but he doesn't. He comes with a groan, nipping at my neck while holding my chin up high.

I expect him to say something, anything. But when he pulls out of me and I sink to my feet, I turn to him walking out of the shower.

My body stills when I take in Cole leaning against the

sink counter. His arms are stretched out, and his knuckles are white as they brace on the countertop as though stopping himself from reaching out. His eyes meet with mine, but I don't see jealousy. I just see need in them, the bulge in his jeans evident.

Jace stands in front of him butt naked before he turns his head over his shoulder and gifts me with a menacing smirk. "She's all yours, brother. Enjoy my sloppy seconds."

I watch in horror when he winks at Cole to antagonize him, but somehow, Cole manages to keep his cool, and when his raging eyes lock on to mine, I shake my head in warning to him.

Jace saunters out of the bathroom, leaving me standing there beneath the flow of the water, never before feeling so dirty and used.

My lip trembles, and as always, my savior rescues me. He scoops me into his arms and hugs me close to him as sobs rack through my body.

I cling to him, and for the first time in my life, I wish Jace Matthews would disappear.

COLE

I held Tia all night as she sobbed into my chest. Her heart broke when that selfish prick used her for his own needs, treating her like shit, then spitting venom out to try and rile me.

The only thing it did was turn me the fuck on. That was until he implied she was just another one of his fuck buddies. He implied he used her, and I won't stand for that.

I get that he's hurt and angry, but none of this is her fault.

None of it. Yet he seems determined to punish her, making me want to protect her all the more.

While Tia sleeps, I tug on my joggers and make my way toward Rage's room. There's no way I'm not having it out with him. Not after last night. I refuse to let him disrespect her.

I swing open his bedroom door to find his bed empty. In fact, it doesn't look like he's slept in it at all this week.

The living and kitchen area are empty too.

"He's in the spare room."

I spin on my heel to find Lucas sipping his coffee as he leans against the wall beside his office door. His gaze travels up and down my body, making me feel unusually hot under his scrutiny. I'm fully aware this gaze feels different. It feels more.

My cock begins to swell in my pants, and the thought makes me swallow hard. Shit, can he see me getting hard? I scrub a hand over my head and avoid eye contact.

"He probably wants to feel close to her," he says.

I latch my eyes on to his, and my stomach somersaults at the thought of my brother hurting for her.

This whole dynamic between us all has got to change. Something has got to give because it's destroying us.

"Just go easy on him, Cole," Lucas warns as I walk toward the spare room.

Opening the door to the room, I step inside; the curtains are still drawn, so it's darker in here than expected, but I can still make out the bottles littering the bedroom floor.

Rage raises his head from the pillow with a wince. "What the fuck do you want?" His voice is scratchy and deadly, but he doesn't scare me.

"You overstepped last night, Rage. You hurt her!"

Rage throws the sheet off him and sits up in bed. "Yeah? Good. I'm pleased I hurt her lying ass." I wince at his words, but knowing he doesn't know the whole story behind Tia makes me hold back. "She's fucking three guys. Who the hell does that?" I grind my jaw as he continues his tirade. "Did you pay her? Is that it? Is she fucking you both for money?"

I stare at him, unblinking; I want to kill him for the words he uses, but through the pain in his eyes, I can see the hurt. I know he loves her. I know he always will. And I also know she loves him too. That's the only reason I'm standing here and letting this shit spew from his mouth without it ending with him needing to have it surgically fixed. He's hurting, and he needs to punish someone. Well, better me than her.

When I don't retaliate, he scans me with shock, as though I'm insane for even taking his words. He wanted a fight, after all.

In the moment, we stare at one another, I swear there's a look of realization passing between us. Neither one of us is prepared to give her up. Neither one of us is prepared to relent. We love her.

We all do.

He raises his chin. "I could make her choose." His dark eyes drill into my unwavering ones.

My heart hammers faster at his words, and panic courses through my veins. Would she pick him?

I try to mask my emotion, but my Adam's apple bobs. "Go for it." I lift my chin back, feigning confidence I don't really feel.

Rage smirks knowingly, making a feeling of sickness whirl in my stomach. I want to scream at him to put a stop to whatever plan he's concocting. Tell him I'll accept anything as long as I'm a part of it. A part of her.

But when he rises and fixes me with his glare, I know there's no talking to him. I know there's no way he'll accept anything other than him and Tia.

"Game on, brother." He smirks.

FIVE

T ia

Cole has been trying to distract me all day. When I first woke up this morning, he made me breakfast in bed, then he ran me a bath, and we've been out all day, and he seems reluctant to take me home.

I clutch his hand as we walk through the mall. "As amazing as today has been, Cole, I've seriously had enough. Can we just go home and watch a movie or something?"

Cole tenses beside me. "We could go to the movies, instead?"

I stop and scan him from head to toe, looking for something out of place or something that's going to explain his behavior today.

"Is something wrong?"

He stares over my shoulder instead of at me, avoiding my eyes. "No. I just figured you'd like to get out."

"Cole, look at me."

With a heavy sigh, he brings his gaze down toward me. He drags a hand over his head, a clear sign he's uncomfortable.

Nervousness fills me, and I fidget with my hands. "Is it . . . is it because of what I did with Jace?" Whatever is happening between me and Jace needs resolving, and soon, before I hurt the very people I love.

Cole's eyes bulge. "What? No. It's not that, I swear. I just . . ." He scans round the mall before his eyes land back on me. He moves closer, and one of his hands tightens on my hip as he leans down. His soft, vulnerable voice sends a shiver over my body. "I don't want to lose you."

My lips drift up to his as though on a magnetic pull. "You won't lose me, I swear it."

His body relaxes into the kiss as he draws me in tighter to him, and I'm forced to cling to him to anchor myself.

That's what Cole does to me. He grounds the raging storm inside me. He anchors me so strongly, even the tsunami of emotions has no power when I'm with him.

LUCAS

The hairs on the back of my neck stand on end, followed by the shadow on the tiles giving him away.

I place the makeup bag back on the counter and choose to ignore his presence. Instead, I deliberately stall and tidy some of the makeup products back into place.

"What the fuck are you doing, Lucas?"

I keep my back to him and sigh heavily, unsure whether to be honest with my intentions or whether to divert his attention once again.

"Lucas. I asked you a goddamn question. What are you doing?"

Turning around slowly, I take in Cole's angry face before ignoring his pissed reaction to me being in their bathroom, and I revert to what I always do. I scan his tight jaw, the way in which it clenches so hard it must bring him pain. His stubble is a day old, and I wonder if it feels good for her when he's between her legs, and finally, I meet his eyes and wonder if he sees more of me like I see more of him.

I slowly drag my tongue over my bottom lip in thought, knowing that Cole is potentially about to explode, so I need to choose my words wisely.

"I swapped out her birth control pills."

His face is blank, and for a moment, I wonder if he hasn't heard me. Then, his eyes bug out before his shoulders bunch tight in aggravation.

"You did fucking what?" His voice is low and deadly. But again, I choose to ignore it.

I stand taller, confident in the choices I've made. "I swapped out her birth control pills."

He stares at me, his face morphed in horror. I lift my shoulder on a shrug. "I want to keep her."

"Keep her?"

I fix my jaw tight because he's acting kind of dumb right now. Does he not understand we're living under the same roof as the love of her life? That at any moment, she could drop us, and we wouldn't have a choice in the matter?

We could lose her forever.

My breath quickens in panic, and I scrub a hand over my heart to ease the dull ache. My throat becomes dry. "I need her," I tell him with certainty.

"You're tricking her," he snipes the words out so abruptly they slice through my thickened skin, causing me to fight back.

"And you're going to lose her. What, you think she's really going to stick around for you?" Cole's face pales, and I ignore the hurt marring his face. "She loves him! She's pined for him for years, Cole. He's her first fucking love, and where the hell does that leave you and me?"

I swear I see his lip quiver, but I refuse to give in now. I need to make him see; this is the only option left for me. For us.

"I can't lose her, Cole. If we have a baby with her . . ." I force my eyes to meet his, hoping he can see the pleading behind them. "She'll need us forever too. Love us forever."

He startles with the realization of my words. "Us?"

I nod, knowing I'm winning him over. Knowing I'm making him see this is the right thing to do. The only thing to do.

He says nothing for a few moments, causing anxiety to ripple through me.

"How long?"

My eyebrows furrow in confusion.

"How long have you been swapping them out?"

I swallow thickly. "Since the beginning."

Cole chokes. "That's . . . that's . . ."

"It's thirteen weeks and five days," I add on to save him from working out how long they've been together and having sex without protection. He's figuring out I swapped them while they were in a relationship, and I wasn't even on the scene.

I was determined, even then, to secure this relationship for them. For us.

Cole swallows heavily. "She could be pregnant now." He chokes the words out in disbelief.

My cock swells at the thought of her pregnant with our child. "She could."

Cole exhales. "Fuck, brother." His words ooze with arousal, making me glance down at his joggers, where his solid cock presses against his waistband.

A silence hangs between us, heavy not just with the knowledge that we're deceiving Tia, but something more. Something dangerously erotic.

He clears his throat. "We're going to watch a movie. You coming to join us?"

Excitement races through my veins at the invitation and the thoughts of securing our future together.

For all of us.

CHAPTER
SIX

T ia
I lay with my head on Cole's lap and my
feet on Lucas's. It's not lost on me I'm in the
very same position I was in not so long ago, when Lucas
could barely touch me. Now, he's drawing lazy circles on
my ankle while Cole plays with my hair.

I sigh contently, my mind focused on the two men
completely devoted to me, but I can't ignore the niggle of
dread at the thought of Jace walking in and seeing us like
this. I know he's hurting, and I'm merely using that hurt
as an excuse for his current behavior. I'm just not sure
how much more I can take.

As if sensing my thoughts, Cole's hand stops moving.
"How about we take this to the bedroom?"

Before I even get a chance to react, Cole has me
thrown over his shoulder, and he smacks my ass so hard
it makes me yelp.

I lift my head as we make our way to his bedroom,

my eyes catching on to Lucas's darkened ones. He smirks in response, sending a tremor through my body, and my clit throbs with anticipation.

Cole throws me on the bed, causing me to bounce with a giggle.

"Jesus, be careful with her!" Lucas snaps, making me sit up on my elbows at his sniping tone. They share a look between them, one I can't figure out, but knowing these two, they're being overprotective.

Lucas drops into the armchair while Cole wastes no time stripping off his T-shirt and joggers. He strokes his cock, the tip glistening and the silver piercing gleaming with his pre-cum.

I sit up to watch him. Wetness pools in my panties, and I take it upon myself to give them a show of their own.

Dragging my camisole over my head, I revel in delight when both men's piercing stares are on me, watching as I squeeze my tits and tug on my nipples.

I bring my fingers to my mouth and suck them in while staring into Cole's heavy eyes.

"Fuck, beauty."

"Take your panties off and give them to Cole." Lucas's voice is laced in need, and my clit throbs at the sound.

I make quick work of removing my panties and hand them to Cole like Lucas instructs.

"Cover your cock and fuck them." His steely eyes latch on to Cole as he uses my panties to cover his cock, then frantically jerks himself off with them.

"Play with your pussy, beauty. Open up and let us see where we're putting our cum."

"Oh god." I moan at his filthy mouth while using both hands to open my slick folds, exposing myself to them. Their eyes burn into me.

"Please," I beg as my fingers find my clit and move with vigor.

Lucas stands and walks toward the edge of the bed beside Cole. He pulls his T-shirt over his head and kicks his joggers to the side. Two gorgeous naked men stare at me, and I can't help but suck in a sharp breath at the sight of them. My mind wanders at how incredible they look together, side by side.

"I want you to fuck her while I fuck her throat," Lucas tells Cole without even sparing him a glance. "I want her head on the edge of the bed."

"You want her on all fours?" Cole's eyes light up while I try and figure out what he's asking. He spins me to face the end of the bed.

They stare at one another; Lucas licks his lips in contemplation. "No."

Cole smirks back at him while I rest my head on the edge of the bed. Lucas looms over me. His darkened eyes sear into me from above, and when Cole's cock is positioned at my opening, I open my mouth wide to accept Lucas's cock.

I close my eyes on a moan as he gently pushes his cock into my mouth, giving me a chance to accept him all the way into the back of my throat. The position is new to me, but I'm also conscious it's all new to Lucas too, and the fact he is finally able to live out all his fantasies with me makes my pussy clench with expectation.

He hisses through his teeth, and his body tightens above me.

"Fuck her hard!" he spits the words to Cole who, up until now, hasn't so much as moved an inch as though waiting for instruction.

COLE

I watch in awe as Lucas slides his cock into her mouth. Her face is partially covered by his body, but her throat is accepting him perfectly, like she was made for him. Made for us.

I rest the tip of my cock at her entrance until Lucas gives me the green light, because I know the second I push into her, I'll have no choice but to fuck her quickly. Already my cock is excited at the thought of coming deep inside her, filling her tender hole with enough cum to make her pregnant. I rest my palm on her flat stomach, and when Lucas grunts, my eyes snap up toward his. We share a look, both completely enthralled at the prospect of her being pregnant with our child.

Since our talk earlier, I've become obsessed with the thought of Tia being pregnant with my baby. Or even Lucas's. It would be ours and a guaranteed way to keep us together, one way or another.

I slide inside her with that thought in mind. Her

warm pussy walls are already tight and wet with arousal, and she clenches me, drawing me in further and making me have to bite my cheek to stop myself from fucking her hard and fast like a feral animal.

"Play with your tits while we fuck you." Lucas's firm, demanding voice pulls my gaze toward him. His back is straight as he slides lazily in and out of her throat. *Fuck me, that's hot.*

Tia pushes her tits together, and like a magnet to her nipples, my lips swoop down and suckle one into my mouth. I flick the ball of my piercing over her peak, and she moans around Lucas's cock.

"Oh fuck. More," he begs.

I slam into her as he closes his eyes and withdraws his cock. It's covered in Tia's saliva, rock hard, and begging for release with pre-cum dripping onto her face. They both pant before he shoves himself back in mercilessly, making her gag and causing his lips to tip into a dark, menacing grin.

My hands move up to her throat, banding around her like a coiled viper. "Fuck. I can feel you, brother." I pant as I slam into her and effectively push him deeper inside her. I move my hands up and down her throat, like I jerk my cock. It feels like he's fucking my hands, and it makes me hungry for the real thing. To feel him and touch him until he snaps.

I squeeze her throat harder, feeling the bulge of his cock down the column of her neck.

"Sooo fucking good." Lucas pants with clenched

teeth. Then he withdraws before he slams back inside, ignoring her splutters.

My balls draw up as our gazes—both filled with desire—lock on one another's.

Both completely devoted to her.

To us.

I squeeze tighter and throw my head back when she convulses around me, my cock pumping deep inside her, each spurt of my cum an opportunity to impregnate her.

"Oh fuck." I slam inside again. "Fuck, yes."

"Tighter, grip it tighter," Lucas chokes out as his cock swells beneath my fingers.

She swallows him down, and I watch in rapture as Lucas comes with my fingers gripping her neck.

His cock.

CHAPTER

SEVEN

Rage
I watch her without her even realizing I'm here, hidden in the shadows of the corridor. She sings along to some music she has playing in her earbuds, and her head bops along with it. She's beautiful, absolutely fucking mesmerizing, and my heart stutters at the thought of having her here.

I've waited so long for this, and now, she's finally here, but I feel like it's being stolen from me. They stole her from me, and I hate them all.

She's so close, yet so far away, and I ache with need for her.

Thalia sighs heavily as she drops the pencil to the table. Clearly, she's hit a stumbling block of some sort. She tugs the earbuds out and throws them on the table before she gets up and walks toward the refrigerator.

I stride toward her with the need to touch her, to pull her into me, and to tell her I'll help her figure out

53

whatever shit she's struggling with, but when I notice the bite mark on her shoulder, anger boils inside me. Rage.

I grip her shoulder and spin her around roughly, too roughly, making her stumble and her ass hit the counter. I grip onto the counter on each side of her, blocking her in. Her chest heaves in shock, and her face flushes at our proximity.

"Who gave you the bite mark?" My tone is menacing, deadly.

She swallows. "I . . . I . . . I'm not sure."

My eyes slam closed, and I breathe through my nostrils to try and control my raging temper over the fact that she doesn't even know who the fuck marked her.

They snap open with venom. "Such a fucking whore."

She winces at my words, and I ignore the tremble passing through her.

"Get on your knees."

Her mouth drops open in shock, and I almost want to laugh at the irony of it.

"Thalia, get on your fucking knees."

I talk slow to her; it's dark, calculated, and laced in hate. Because that's what she does to me. She brings out my darkness and drowns in it with me.

"What's wrong, baby? I'm not good enough for you?" I purposely make my tone sarcastic and mocking. I'm trying to hurt her; I'm trying to push her. I want her to know how much I hate her.

Her teary eyes meet mine. "Is that what you want, Jace? Is that what you need to feel better? To stop the hurting?" She drops to her knees between me and the counter, and her mouth snaps open for me to use.

My pulse races. *Is* this what I want? To use her like this? As I stare down at the beautiful girl before me, guilt slices into my heart, but it's quickly diminished when I see their mark on her.

I mask my feelings with a sneer and unbuckle my jeans with haste before I change my mind. Lifting my heavy cock from my boxers, excitement builds inside me when she widens her eyes. I've grown a lot since the last time Thalia took me in her mouth, and I marvel at the thought of her touching me like that again. I stare down at her on her knees worshipping me. So fucking beautiful.

I hold the tip of my cock to her lips. "Kiss it."

She glares at me before moving forward and doing just that. My balls draw up at her tender touch, and it angers me that I feel like coming already.

"Lick the slit."

Her tongue does as I instruct, and my eyes roll at the overwhelming sensation. Fuck me, she's incredible.

Gripping her hair tightly in one hand and my cock in the other, I feed myself into her mouth. Her warm slick tongue dances over my sensitive head, and when she runs her tongue over my slit again, I grind my teeth in desperation. I quickly withdraw, my chest panting.

This is what she does to me; she makes me lose control. She's already stolen my mind, and now, she's stealing my control too.

She's taken every. Fucking. Thing. From. Me.

I slam into her and withdraw.

"Fucking." *Slam.* "Hate." *Withdraw.* "You." *Slam.*

I'm on the verge of coming, so I quickly withdraw, and like the bastard I am, I jerk my cock over her face, my balls tightening so fucking hard it hurts. I come with a roar, spilling my cum over her beautiful face, marking her as mine.

I stare at her face mixed with cum and tears, and my heart aches. Cole is right when he calls her beauty. But she's mine!

I pull back and quickly tuck my cock away. Avoiding the hurt in her eyes, I go for the kill, because I just can't seem to help myself. "Tell your boyfriends they're welcome to lick it up."

I storm out of the apartment and head toward the club with the need to let off some aggression before I lose my goddamn mind.

TIA

Lucas has been in his office all day, and Cole has been at the gym. Apparently, he's training some guy for a fight tonight, so he'll be home late.

After Jace used me this morning in the kitchen, I made a pact with myself that I wouldn't allow it to happen again. He can't keep treating me the way he is. As much as he's hurting, I am too. But I can't carry on like this, and the thought of bringing Harper here while this turmoil is happening terrifies me.

I've even started to think about getting my own place but then I know I'll be hurting Cole and Lucas. Either way, we're screwed, and someone will get hurt.

I place Cole's socks in his drawer and turn when I hear the door click shut. I expect to see Lucas standing there, but instead, I'm met with a bloodied Jace. My lip wobbles when I take in his face. His lip is split, and his eye is swollen. I scan his body and find his knuckles are busted too. I suck in a sharp breath as emotion clogs my throat.

"Hey, it's okay. Don't get upset, baby." Jace's gentle tone is completely unlike the one from earlier; it's like before . . . I wince at the memory.

His hand breezes over my arm, causing goose bumps to cover my body like a second skin. I haven't realized I'm crying until Jace drags his thumb over my cheek and wipes away the tears. The tender act tugs at my heart, and I ache for the Jace of my past.

The moment between us is heavy but short-lived when he takes a step back, disconnecting from the tender moment, disconnecting from me.

He drags a hand through his hair "You, err . . . you fancy wrapping these?" He stretches out his hands with a playful smile, one that lights up his whole face and sends flutters running through me.

"Of course." I nod toward the bathroom, and he follows me inside.

Jace pulls himself up to sit on the counter. He watches me closely as I gather up the cream, bandages, and tape for his ruined knuckles.

I rip open the bandage and place it down on the counter. Taking a hold of his hand, I take in his tattoos, even his fingers are covered with the words "Heart Broke" written across them. Pain lances my chest, and my body stills at the reminder of what we became for one another. Pain.

I gently smear the cream over his knuckles.

"I remember you used to do this a lot for me." He chuckles sadly.

My spine straightens at the reminder of our past, how quickly Jace would move to protect me.

"Remember the time I kicked that dipshit Derek's ass who asked you out on a date?"

I giggle at the memory, biting into my lip. "It was not a date, it was to study."

Jace laughs playfully and shakes his head.

"And his name was David, not Derek."

He rolls his eyes. "What. The. Fuck. Ever. He wanted in your panties."

I gasp in horror. "He was gay, Jace. Gay, meaning he didn't want in my panties."

He chokes on a mocking laugh. "That's what he told you."

I wrap his hands with the bandage tightly, one after the other.

"No, you just thought every guy was after me and my panties."

"That's because you're fucking beautiful."

I still at his words, my pulse races, and a flush creeps over my face as he scans over me, not a glimmer of hate in sight.

Only admiration. Devotion.

"Leave them." His words are soft as they leave his lips on a gentle, heartfelt whisper, laced in a begging plea, making my heart constrict at the torment behind his voice.

His eyes implore mine, but I refuse to acknowledge

the desperation behind his. He takes my hands in his. "Please, Thalia."

I wince at his desperation.

I withdraw my hand and slide it down his sharp jawline. How I've longed to touch him once again. Jace leans into me, his dark eyes filled with love. I glance away, unable to see him want me so much.

My eyes blur with tears, and my body shakes with anxiousness as I rise to meet his face. I answer truthfully, knowing I'm going to hurt him all over again. "I can't."

He sucks in a sharp breath, his face crumbles, and his Adam's apple bobs as he tugs his hands from mine.

Jumping down from the counter, he steps aside. "I get it. You prefer two cocks instead of one, right?" He's back to hating me, and I steel myself for the vitriol about to come.

"I love them, Jace."

He flinches.

"I love you too." My eyes plead with his to make him realize how much I do care for him.

His lip trembles, then he sets his mask in place. "Me or them."

I can't respond. My mind won't work. Is he really making me choose? Giving me an ultimatum?

"Me or them, Thalia?" His voice booms, making me startle. "Me. Or. Fucking. Them!"

It feels like my soul is being ripped from me; it's being destroyed in front of my very eyes, and I'm powerless to do anything. The boy I fell in love with or the men I've grown to love?

Silence.

My heart thuds so in my chest so strong I can hear it in my ears.

"Them."

My chest hurts with the strength behind my heartbeat leaving me breathless as I await his reaction.

He chokes, then licks his lips. His downcast head rises with a new purpose in mind. "Right." I flinch at his brutal tone, the way his eyes bore into mine with malice. "Right," he repeats as though talking to himself.

I move to comfort him, but he steps away. Turning, he leaves me alone in the bathroom, and finally, my knees buckle as I give way to devastation in a crumpled heap, knowing I've broken his heart all over again.

EIGHT

L ucas

Tia picks at her meal, pushing the pasta from one side of the plate to the other. My fists clench with a need to comfort her, but I'm unsure how.

I don't know what Rage said or did, but I know he hurt her, and the need to hurt him back is almost too much to bear.

We've been so close since he first came to live with us. He seemed to understand my demons and respected them like a true brother. Cole originally joked that we were brothers, but I saw the glimmer of hope—the need to have a family—in Rage's eyes when he said it, because it was mirrored in mine.

He wanted to belong somewhere, he needed a family to love him, and he had that in us. The only thing missing was her.

I was determined to find her for him.

I just never expected us all to fall for her.

"Maybe I should move out?"

My heart jackknives. Absolutely fucking not. "No."

"It hurts him, me being here, Lucas. I can't hurt him." Tears stream down her face. "It hurts me," she admits.

"You're not leaving. I'll speak to him." My tone leaves no room for argument, and she nods back at me, uncertainty coating her features.

Panic bubbles in my veins, and I clench my hand around my knife and stroke over the wood soothingly to reassure myself.

"Do you want to watch a movie?" I ask on a hopeful whim because I have no clue what to do right now.

Tia's face breaks out into a delicate smile, already simmering the raging storm inside me. "Sure."

I can't focus on the movie, not at all. I need to fix this. For her. For him. Us.

Staring down at Tia's face on my lap, I stroke over her silky hair again, loving being able to freely touch her like this. Tia whimpers in her sleep, and the sound makes my blood freeze with a need to protect and comfort her.

"It's okay. I've got you," I whisper, and at the sound of my voice, her body melts against mine, leaving me with a feeling of satisfaction.

"Shall we get you to bed?"

"Mm hm. Can you carry me?" She smiles with her eyes still closed, making me smile at her adorable response.

Tugging her to my chest, I rise to my feet and head toward Cole's bedroom.

There's a fumble at the apartment door, making my eyes shoot over toward it. It's too early to be Cole, and when Jace went storming out earlier, I assumed he wouldn't be back tonight. There's giggling, and a bolt of awareness hits me. He wouldn't, would he?

Tia slides down my chest, her feet landing on the wood floor with a thud as we stare at the doorway in shock.

Rage strolls into the apartment, his eyes unfocused, so he's clearly drunk, but it's the girl who's attached to him that I can't tear my eyes away from. She's the same girl he was with when Cole and I collected him from the club, and she's all over him right now. His arm is draped over her, and she nuzzles into his neck with a hand roaming beneath his T-shirt.

I cringe at the intoxicated state of them, but when his gaze fixes on Tia, I know the bastard set this up. He means for her to see every kiss and caress this girl gives him.

Tia's face pales, and I feel her shudder beside me. The sharp inhale of breath shows she's struggling to keep herself together, and I want to fucking kill him for it.

They breeze past us, his hand gripping the girl's ass, who hasn't so much as acknowledged our existence, but just as he gets toward his bedroom door, he glances over his shoulder with a smirk. "Have a good night, I know I'm going to." He winks at us, causing Tia to jolt. "Come on, baby, show me what you've got."

The use of Tia's nickname slices through my heart, so I can only imagine what it's doing to hers.

Rage has hit the point of no return, and I'm torn between storming into his room and demanding he stop doing whatever it is he's about to do or completely ignoring him and comforting the girl whose heart he's breaking. The decision is taken out of my hands when Tia slips her trembling hand into mine.

"Can you hug me tonight?" Her tear-filled eyes meet mine.

My Adam's apple bobs. "Of course." I stare at her with my heart thundering in my chest and a need to reassure her consuming me. "I love you."

It's pitiful compared to how I feel, when I want to take away every bit of her pain—past, present, and future—but I leave it hanging there for her to latch on to, when beyond the door, a shriek of giggles are destroying her.

"I love you too." My shoulders relax at her words, and without thinking, I bend down and scoop her up, letting her head fall against the strong beat of my heart.

"It's going to be okay." I press kisses into her hair as I kick open Cole's bedroom door, and finally, when the door clicks shut, her sobs give way and so does her heart.

JACE

The fake blonde shrieks in delight when I pick her up and launch her onto my bed. All night she's been flirting with me and dragging her talons over my body, making my skin crawl in disgust. But I'm determined to rid myself of this need for Thalia.

She thinks it's okay to fuck two guys and, what, fuck me too? Screw that, she's meant to be mine.

The blonde crawls up the bed toward me, and already, I want to wash off her touch. I lean back on my pillows with a hand behind my head, determined to get into this and over the need for Thalia that consumes every fiber of my being.

"Take your top off," I snap in her direction, and without any finesse, the blonde attempts to take her top off. She catches her hair while attempting to pull it over her head, but eventually, with a struggle, she pulls her head through the hole and drops her top to the floor. Her purple lipstick is smeared on her teeth, and as I take in her bedraggled state, I can't find anything remotely attractive about her.

There's nothing natural looking, nothing like Thalia. And with that awareness, I realize I've been holding every woman at a distance; I've purposely been avoiding anyone I could have a future with because in my heart, I was holding out for *her*.

She crawls over my body and starts grinding down on my soft cock, and the urge to knock her off me makes me grind my teeth. As if realizing my lack of arousal, she starts moaning loudly, making me cringe at the thought that the whole apartment will hear this. Hear her.

A flash of Thalia's heartbroken face surges into me, making my body involuntarily shudder at the hurt I've purposely caused. Of course the blonde thinks the shudder is one of arousal and bounces on my dick like she's on a bucking bronco.

I close my eyes and try to imagine it's Thalia, but all I see is the hurt reflecting back at me. The same hurt I saw when I left her five years ago.

"Stop!" I bark and then scrub a hand through my hair when she doesn't get the memo. "Yo, blondie. Chill the fuck out." She stops, with her mouth agape. I blow out a deep breath. "You're gonna have to go." I pick her up and place her on the floor while she stares at me with a stunned expression on her face.

"I was about to suck your cock."

Her words stop me. Oh hell no! I don't want her anywhere near my cock; her last attempt wasn't worth it, and I sure as hell can't imagine this would be either. Not when I know the only girl I'll ever want is currently down the hall hating my guts.

I grab her bag from the floor and push it into her chest.

"Are you gay?"

I stop in my tracks because, what the hell?

"You're gay, right? That's why you don't want this." She throws her arm out and trails it over her body in a move that's meant to be seductive.

My eyes widen at her assertation of my rejection. "No, darlin', I'm not gay."

She scoffs. "I heard it takes you ages to get off. I had a bet running tonight I could make you come in five minutes." She blows on her nails and throws her hair over her shoulder.

This time, it's my turn to scoff. "Sweetheart, you couldn't make me come if I gave you five months. That's why I figured I'd save us both the time and effort." I shrug, trying to act nonchalant to the fact that I—and my lack of coming skills—have been spoken about. I'm not even going to lie and pretend I haven't fucked every woman, every face to the image of Thalia. And when I finally have her in reach, I fuck it up for the shitty replacement standing in front of me glaring daggers of contempt in my direction.

"You can pay my cab fare."

I tug my wallet out of the back of my jeans pocket, relieved I'm managing to get rid of her without a fight. Truth be told, I figured those nails would become claws and she'd try digging them in firmly.

I swing open my bedroom door and watch with amusement as she sashays down the hall and out of the apartment door.

I close my bedroom door and bang my head repeatedly against it. What a fucking idiot.

Now I need to pull my shit together, and whatever this thing is between Thalia and me, I need to make it work.

I can't lose her. Not again.

CHAPTER
NINE

Tia

I swirl the spoon in the mug of hot chocolate numbly. My mind feels blank and part of my heart empty. Part of me.

Warmth spreads across my back, and his scent invades me, making my spine straighten. The breeze of his breath flutters over my face as he angles his head toward my ear.

"I'm sorry."

I swallow thickly at his words but choose to ignore them.

Jace sighs heavily. "I didn't fuck her."

I jolt and try to step back, but he brackets his hands on either side of the counter, locking me in.

"I don't care anymore, Jace." My voice sounds sad, defeated, even to my own ears.

He freezes. "Thalia, listen to me."

I shake my head, refusing to take any more.

"Please, fucking listen to me."

His begging tone forces a sob to catch in my throat, and before I know what's happening, he's spinning me around to face him. His fingers graze my chin, lifting my face, no doubt seeing the tears streaming down my cheeks. "Jesus, baby. I'm sorry."

I close my eyes at his words, refusing to listen. I won't be drawn in by him. Not again.

"I'm not doing this with you, Jace."

I feel him tense and immediately sense the anger radiating off him. I tremble, waiting for him to burst into a tirade of fury.

He lifts me, and when I open my eyes, I'm being flung over his shoulder as he strides toward his bedroom.

"Jace? What the hell?"

"You won't listen to me. So I'll show you."

He slams the door shut behind us and drops me on the edge of his bed. Taking in his room, I cringe at his missing bed sheets, and a wave of sickness overwhelms me.

"I didn't fuck her, Thalia." Jace brushes his hand over his already messy hair. "I just wanted everything that touched her gone."

I snap my eyes up. "You let her touch you."

He licks his lips while staring down at me. Then, he lifts his shirt, exposing his toned tattooed stomach. Jace drags a hand over his abs. "I scrubbed myself." I take in the raised redness and wince before lifting my head to find him swallowing harshly. "I scrub myself after every . . . encounter."

My heart hammers hard in my chest, and jealousy swirls deep in my stomach. I hold a hand up to stop him from speaking, refusing to recognize that he's been with other women.

Once again, I feel the shift in him, the rage. He takes a step back to glare at me. "You know how long it took me to be with someone else, Thalia?" His gentle tone is gone. He breathes through his nostrils, his chest rising in annoyance. "Eighteen fucking months before I could as much as touch another woman!"

His voice rises in anger, and I snap, jumping to my feet. "You're unbelievable, you know that?" He scans my face in confusion. "You want me to pity you? Because you didn't fuck another woman for eighteen months? Are you serious?"

"I don't need your fucking pity, Thalia. I need you to understand."

"I understand I hate the fact you've been with other women, Jace. When we promised one another only us. I understand that I don't like the fact you only waited eighteen months before you had sex with someone else. I also understand that it took me five fucking years to get there, and yet, you've been there this whole damn time."

He stares at me like I'm a madwoman before something clicks inside him, and his shoulders sag with the realization.

"You never fucked anyone else?"

I wince, a wave of sickness rolls over me again, and my body begins to shake as I close the memories down.

His rough hand brushes over my arm, gently caressing me, anchoring me to the present.

"I've only been with them." I lift my chin. "They're it for me." I let my words hit him, hoping they churn his stomach like he has mine. Yet still a part of me wants him to fight for us.

He reaches up to my neck, and when I expect his palm to press on my throat, he yanks the chain off my neck and walks toward his closet.

I watch him as he tugs a wooden chest out of the closet, the same one he had in his room back in our foster home.

Walking over to me, he takes my hand in his and places the small key into my palm. He nods toward the chest. "It's all yours."

I stare at the chest in uncertainty as Jace takes a seat in the armchair beside his bed.

Walking over to the chest, I kneel down grazing my fingers over the wooden craftsmanship. I ease the key into the lock, unsure of what to expect.

The lid springs open and reveals books upon books, piled neatly. I lift one out, and it's then I realize they're journals.

Jace's journals.

My fingers trail over the messy handwriting, and I flick open the first page.

Jace Matthews loves Thalia Knight
Aged thirteen

October Thirty-first.

Thalia woke me this morning with a candle on a cupcake. I'm officially a teenager. I hate it already. I can't wait to turn eighteen and get away from this place.

Me and Thalia dressed as clowns and pranked that prick Martin with toilet paper shoved in his car exhaust. I told Thalia I'd take the blame and say me and one of my soccer buddies did it if he ever finds the clown masks.

December Twenty-fifth

I watched Thalia open her present. I wrapped it myself, and it looks pretty damn good with a green bow on top to match the sweater she loves so much.

She wasn't expecting me to get her anything, but I saved up all my money from the summer job I took cutting lawns to get her the same pad and pencils she uses in art.

Tears well in my eyes as I pull out another journal.

April Twelfth

Zeke deserved that fist to his mouth. If he says another damn thing about my girl's rack, I swear I'm going to make him regret it.

I've been bulking up, so I know I can take him. I might be fourteen, but I look older. I know that.

I saw Thalia watching me when I walked out of the bathroom today. My dick was rock hard, and I couldn't swallow. My whole damn body froze like an idiot.

Her face went bright red. So cute.

January fourth

I had to bribe David to get Thalia a shift at the store on the same day as me. That way I can walk her to and from home.

When she was stacking the shelves, her jeans dipped low, and I swear I saw some ass.

I jerked off all night to how tight I imagine her ass being. I can't wait until summer when I get to see her in her swimmers.

I'll kill anyone who looks at her.

My heart pounds at the memories assaulting me. All the years of wanting and waiting for one another.

I take out another journal.

July Twelfth

I asked her to the dance. Even though she isn't sixteen yet, she looks it. Besides, I don't care what my friends say. She belongs to me.

I see the way they look at her. Desperate for her.

She's mine. Always has been, always will be.

September First

She went on a fucking date!

With that piece of shit Clint. What the fuck kind of name is Clint anyway?

My knuckles hurt so fucking bad from punching the wall. Then, that shit, Martin hit me in the head because of it.

I hate him.

September Second

She didn't kiss him. I didn't even have to ask her, she just told me outright.

She wrapped my knuckles up, and I swear, my dick got hard just from her touch.

I wanted to kiss her.

So bad.

January Fourteenth

So fucking grateful it's cold.

Thalia asked me to stay in her room again last night.

When she shoves her ass against my dick, I have to think of a million things to stop my dick going hard.

I choke on a laugh when I consider how many times I shoved my ass against his dick, hoping for a reaction. Swiping the tears from my eyes, I continue reading.

April Fifth

I touched her tit last night, and she fucking moaned.

Moaned.

I swear, I almost came in my pants.

April Twelfth

I kissed her. I finally fucking kissed her.

It was incredible.

May Thirteenth
My scholarship came through. I feel fucking sick.
She told me I have to do it. This way, we can be together forever if we can just get past her last year of high school.

Emotion clogs my throat as I remember this day, the bittersweet memory of him achieving his dreams for us and yet me knowing my nightmares were about to start. My hell.

June Eighteenth
Martin keeps staring at her. He doesn't even try to disguise it. I swear, he's doing it on purpose just to rile me up.

My body shakes, knowing he saw the way he looked at me. If only we could have done more. I glance over my shoulder at Jace to see him watching me closely, his dark eyes trained on me as he nibbles at his fingernail nervously. I can see him struggling to rein in the need to comfort me, but he knows how important this is. I need to see this, see his own battle, his own struggles and demons. Maybe this way, we can face mine.

August First
I've saved up enough to buy her a cell phone to use while I'm away. That way, we can stay in contact.
I know she's worried about other girls, but how the fuck can I look at anyone else? All I see is her.

I never received the cell phone. I hiccup away the tears, knowing the effort he made.

August Twelfth
My fists are bleeding again. I swear, I hate him. He was in her room. Why the fuck would a grown man be in her room? He's our foster father.
I've warned him not to touch her.
I'll kill him.

I squeeze my eyes shut, forcing away the memory of his invasion of my privacy. I always knew when he'd been in there. Knew when he'd been watching.

August Thirteenth
I can't write. I can't write because I can't fucking see through tears. I'm crying like a goddamn pussy.

It was amazing.

Absolutely fucking amazing.

I gave her the key to these diaries. One day, she can look back and see how long I've loved her.

A lifetime.

I choke on a sob, my eyes now so blurry, I have to stop to pull myself together.

August Nineteenth

She isn't answering her phone.

I haven't been gone a week, and already, she isn't answering.

She promised.

August twenty-first

Every minute feels like a year, everyday like a lifetime.

Where the hell is she?

September First

I bet she's with that little prick Zeke.

I punched the wall so hard, I broke two knuckles.

I've never felt such anger and heartache.

She promised.

I wish I could tell him how much I wanted him to rescue me.

How much he must have been hurting when he wrote this.

September Twelfth
I called my buddy Troy to check in on her.
He said she's been quiet and not been at school for ages.
I'm worried she's sick. What if she needs me?

October Eighteenth
I hate it here. I actually want to go home. Back to hell just to be with her.
I can't think straight. Can't concentrate. I'm going to flunk, I know it.
I smashed up my room.
I need her to wrap up my knuckles.

He needed me, and I wasn't there. Pain hits me in my chest, forcing me to suck in a deep breath.

"Baby?" Jace moves from the chair, but I hold up my hand to stop him.

"Please. I need to do this."

He slowly eases back into the chair but leans forward on his elbows as though trying to be as close as possible.

November First

I'm broken. She didn't even call on my birthday.

I couldn't leave the room just in case she called. I've wrote her a letter every week in case he found her cell phone. I called the house, and the number is dead.

It's like she's disappeared from my life.

I've no reason to be here without her.

She's the reason I live.

November Thirteenth

I persuaded Cole to drive me the six hours to check on her.

The house is empty.

She's gone.

It's like she never existed.

December twelfth

Cole found me passed out with a bunch of pills and an empty bottle of whiskey. I don't know what I was thinking.

That's a lie.

I was thinking about her.

I ball my fists and let out a wail. He was in his own hell. While I was in mine, he was in his.

January First
I wonder if she watched the fireworks last night?
When a girl came over and touched my neck, I wanted to throw up.
I can't be with anyone else but her.
I hate her for doing this to me, to us.
Making me fall in love with her then stealing my heart.
Destroying it.

February second
For my twentieth birthday, Cole and Lucas are on a mission to "Break me out of her spell." We have a business plan to start our own fight club.
When we make enough money, I'm going to track her down.
I'm going to make her pay for hurting me like this.

This is where he hates me?

I hate her.

This huge hole gapes in the center of my heart. Growing bigger by the day.

Why did she do this? Blocked all contact. Discarded me so easily when my life is so consumed by her.

Didn't she see how much she meant to me?

Aged Twenty-one.
June eleventh
I wonder if she still loves ketchup and mayo mixed together.
If her hair is still silky.
If when she kisses, she moans.
I wonder if she still thinks of me.

He still loves me. He never stopped thinking of me. Never stopped wanting me.

I turn to finally face him. Tears flow down his face with a look of vulnerability shining through them, but his eyes never stray from mine. "I love you, Thalia. Always have. Always will."

T ia

Jace peppers kisses down my face before gently suckling the skin on my neck into his mouth and tugging, no doubt marking me, but I can't find it in me to care right now.

"You still taste and smell as good as I remember. Fuck, baby, does your pussy still taste good?"

He continues his descent. Lifting my top from over my head, he takes in my breasts. Pushing them together, he massages my nipples into peaks, making me moan at the sensation.

"Fuck, they grew nice and big." He pushes them together, then stills when he notices the red mark left behind by Lucas.

He swallows deeply, making me freeze at what his reaction is going to be. He ducks his head, and relief floods me when he angles his mouth over the mark only to suck it harder, marking me further.

I can only imagine it's his way of defeating them. His way of showing them I belong to him too. I push up into him, dragging my fingers through his hair and tugging it sharply when his teeth graze my nipple.

"Jesus, Jace. You feel so good. I need you."

He leans back on his heels, tugs his shirt from over his head, and lowers his joggers.

"Do you let them fuck you without protection?" He tugs on his cock and pre-cum leaks in a sticky trail over his palm.

"I'm on the pill." My voice is breathy as I watch in awe of his nakedness, taking in every inch of his tattooed body.

"I'm clean. I've only ever fucked my girl without a condom." His chest rises as he fists himself harder. "Only ever fucked the one girl who has my heart without a condom." I nod at his words.

"Slide your panties off and open your pussy for me."

I work quickly, lowering my panties and throwing them to the floor. I sit up and watch as his eyes become heavy when I separate my slick folds, allowing him to see me open and exposed for him.

"Fuck, your juices are running out your hole, baby. I need to fuck it back in so bad." His fist pumps faster, and his hips start to move.

An urge to have him inside me takes over, and just like the day he made love to me, my mouth runs away from me, gifting him with this filthy side of me reserved purely for Jace.

"I want to feel your cock inside me, Jace, stretching my pussy. I want to feel you pump your cum inside me." I move one hand to my breast and tweak my sensitive nipple. "Please stretch me."

"Fuck, baby. Fuck." Jace moves quickly, falling on top of me, he surges inside. His open mouth finds mine as I take his thick cock all the way to the base, stretching me. I lie stunned until his tongue invades my mouth. Thrashing about like a wild animal, he groans when he pulls out and slams back in. I claw at his back; it's hard and fast, messy and desperate. It's passion, it's everything.

"More," I beg on a moan.

"Fuck yes. Beg me for my cum. Beg me like you beg them."

I can't help but flinch at his words, not because of anything other than the fact he's been listening to us, but the hint of a jealous crack in his voice makes me clench tightly around him, eager to hold him inside me.

"Fuck, tell me you love it."

I hold on to his tattooed body plowing roughly into my pussy while I squirm beneath him. "Oh fuck, Jace. I love you fucking me hard."

He rears back, his eyes shining brightly as they roam over my body as though gobsmacked that it's me below him.

"You're like a fucking vision, Thalia." He slams into me. "You're all my fucking dreams come true." *Slam.* "You're it for me, baby." *Slam.* "You're it!"

I throw my head back and scream as I squeeze his cock, milking it for both our pleasures. He swells inside me, his hips still moving as my body flutters high on the adrenaline.

When he finally falls on top of me, his lips find mine, a tender kiss, a contrast to his frantic fucking.

"I love you, Thalia."

"I love you too."

He gently strokes the hair from my eyes. "We're going to make this work, baby." He swallows past a lump, and his face fills with uncertainty. I hold him tighter, already concerned he's withdrawing. "I just . . . I can't watch you fucking them."

He spits the words out, and I nod in understanding, because truth be told, I couldn't handle that if it was him. "I understand."

"I know you love them, but—" He swallows hard. "Do you think you could love me the same way too?"

My lips tremble, and my heart breaks for him. How can he possibly think otherwise? "I've loved you every day from the moment I laid eyes on you, Jace. That never stopped, not once."

"But . . ."

I shake my head, not wanting to go into the wheres and whys of how it all went wrong. How we went wrong.

"I love you. Is that enough for you?" I question him, holding my breath.

"It's everything." His body relaxes against me, and when his lips find mine and his cock begins to harden, I know I wouldn't want to be anywhere else other than where I am right now.

Jace was right; this is a dream, and I ignore the fact that I hold nightmares set to haunt us both.

JACE

I take Tia's hand in mine and lead her out of my bedroom. I'm not sure how this is going to work between us, but it will work, because I refuse to lose her.

After I fucked her hard, I made love to her, then we showered together, something I've only ever been able to dream about doing until now.

We're going to have to come up with some damn schedule or something because now that I have her, I don't want to spend a damn night away from her, and I can guaran-fucking-tee that Lucas and Cole will be feeling the same way.

But we need to make it work, for all our sakes.

Cole and Lucas are sitting at the dining table when we walk in. They stop talking and raise their heads, eyes locking on to our hands and then our faces. Cole breaks out into a huge smile and sits back smugly in his chair with his hands behind his head while Lucas scans over Tia as though checking she's unharmed. I see the moment he realizes one of his marks on the side of her neck has now been expanded and is marked by me instead. *Yes, motherfucker, how do you like that?*

I smirk at him, and he rolls his eyes. "Nice to see you have your shit together." He glares at me when I pull out a chair and lift Thalia onto my lap. "Finally," he tacks on at the end, earning him a chuckle from Cole.

My nostrils flare in annoyance. How the fuck dare he after he was the one who ruined it all? "Well, if someone didn't try and steal her from me in the first place . . ." Thalia elbows me in the ribs, and I stop before I fuck everything up.

"As much as I'd like to hang around you lovebirds today, I have training to do." Cole stands and leans over the table to grab an apple. "What's the plan with Harper tomorrow?"

My eyes narrow in confusion at what I've missed, but the way Thalia tenses on me, I know it's something big.

Before I get to ask her, she opens her mouth and explains, "Harper's my daughter."

All the world stands still, as though we're frozen. Because I think she just said she has a daughter.

Then, the room begins to spin. I'm vaguely aware that Thalia is standing above me and talking to me, but I can't hear her. All I hear are her words from our earlier argument.

I also understand that it took me five fucking years to get there.

And now, it all makes sense. She has a daughter, and

I'm a fucking father? My chest swells with pride as I snap out of my shock.

"I have a daughter?"

Her face pales, and she looks on the verge of passing out. Her body begins to shake, and when I stand, she backs away from me.

Lucas moves behind her, holding her up. What the fuck is happening?

"She's not yours, brother." Cole drags his hand awkwardly over his head, his words low and full of sympathy.

I startle at his words; anger floods my veins. She lied to me.

"You lied to me!" my voice bounces off the walls so loudly, the room becomes silent, apart from Thalia's hiccuping sob. "You. Fucking. Lied. To. Me."

She shakes her head. "I didn't, I swear, I didn't."

But I refuse to listen. "You bitch. You fucking bitch."

Cole lunges at me, his fist cracking into my jaw. Lucas lets go of Thalia and steps between us, pushing me against the wall away from Cole. Our chests heave in fury at one another.

"I didn't choose to sleep with anyone, Jace. I would never." She squeezes her eyes shut, but the pain is written all over her face.

"What the fuck's she talking about?" I dart my eyes over to Lucas. "Lucas!" I snap because nobody is telling me a damn thing.

Thalia's eyes flare open with confidence, a stark

95

contrast to only a few seconds ago. She steels her spine and says, "Martin forced himself on me."

Time suspends at her words, and my body feels heavy as my stomach lurches. Please no.

"But she's my daughter." Thalia stabs her finger at her chest for emphasis. "Mine."

I slide down the wall.

I didn't protect her.

When I thought I was living in hell, she truly was, and I chose to ignore it.

CHAPTER

ELEVEN

Tia
I watch in tortured silence as Jace slides down the wall, his ass landing on the floor with a thud and his face contorting with a mixture of horror and devastation. He drops his head into his hands and rocks back and forth with choked sobs.

Memories assault me from every direction.

Five years ago . . .

I can't stomach any breakfast this morning. Not when I know what's about to happen. Not when my life is going to change into a living hell.

Jace walks into my bedroom with his backpack over his shoulder, and I can't so much as raise my head to greet him.

My heart is breaking, and I can't let him see. Can't let him feel the terror and heartbreak building inside me.

He drops his bag to the floor and kneels beside me. Using his fingers, he raises my chin to stare back into his stormy eyes, the same ones that made love to me last night and again this morning.

"I love you, baby." His words give me strength but also fill my eyes with grateful tears. I nod at his words, unable to find my own to reassure him.

He clears his throat and digs into his jeans pocket. "Here, I have this for you." He opens his palm to gift me with a small gold key attached to a thin necklace.

"What is it?"

"The key to my heart, what do you think?" He smirks at me, making me smack his arm playfully. "I'll tell you what it is when you graduate. I just want you to know, I'll be thinking of you always."

"I love you," I blurt the words out as he rises to his feet.

Jace smiles down at me like I'm his whole world, then steps away and walks out the door, taking the only happiness I have with him.

I can't help the wail that leaves my lips as the car door slams outside.

And only when the familiar sickening feeling of being watched penetrates my mind do I let myself stop crying.

His tall body fills the door—my only escape from hell—as he steps further into the room, his shadow creeping alongside him.

"You've nobody to keep you safe now, Thalia. No hero to rescue you. You belong to me now, buttercup." He licks his lips like a predator preparing to devour its prey, and I close my eyes and beg for time to run away with me.

Beg for my graduation so I can be free with Jace.

Beg for mercy.

CHAPTER

TWELVE

Jace

I don't even know how I ended up in bed next to her. Her soft lips flutter on each exhale as I watch her sleeping form in rapture.

She's beyond anything I've ever witnessed before, and I'm so fucking lucky to claim her as mine, even if I have to share her with them.

My heart hammers, and nausea washes over me the moment I realize the girl I love and lost was hurt. No, not just hurt, brutalized. By the man who made it his mission to make every day in that house a living hell for me.

My mind wanders back in time, a time I've fought so damn hard to block out.

"You're a little punk, you know that?!" Martin screams so close to my face spittle hits my cheek. "You're going to stand against this wall and watch me eat dinner because pieces of shit like you don't deserve food when they waste it."

When I accidently dropped my plate with the meatloaf on it, Martin flew up from his chair like a madman.

My fists clench at my side. I hate him so damn much. "If Thalia hadn't cleaned it up so quick, I'd have made you lick it off the floor like last week." He grins at me manically, and I imagine pummeling his face until he's bloody and unrecognizable.

I know Thalia cleaned it up quickly to save me the embarrassment. She always does that, trying to defend me, and in return, I try and protect her, from scum like him and his friends that come over to watch football and treat us like slaves.

I turn my head toward the dining table and Thalia flinches as he sits beside her. She hates him being so close. Even I know that, and I'm only eleven. How the hell has he not worked it out too?

My pulse races as flashback after flashback hit me, making it impossible for me to breathe quietly.

"You either chop the fucking wood, or I'll make Thalia do it, and you know she whined like a little bitch over her hands the last time, don't you?"

She didn't whine, she was fucking brave, and I loved her for it. He wouldn't let her use gloves, and he said he'd hit me in the stomach again if she didn't carry on. But I took the choice away from her, pushing over the tin of paint on the porch with the tip of my toe. He went crazy.

I crept into her room when he was asleep and helped her pick the splinters of wood from her palms, and she lathered my back in lotion from the cane he used.

I lift the axe and slam it down hard, imagining I'm chopping the prick's head off.

One day, Martin. One day.

All this time, I thought I was able to protect her from the worst of it, but clearly, it was a living hell for her too.

One I left her in.

I need to make him pay, and with those thoughts in my mind, I slide out of the sheets and make my way toward Lucas's office.

I'm not shocked to find Cole in there too, and their heads turn when I walk in and fold my arms over my chest defensively.

"I need to know everything," I say to Lucas, because clearly, the prick has been holding out on me. He knows a lot more than he admits, and by the way he jolts and pales, I know whatever he does know, I'm not going to like.

"You best sit down." He points to the couch opposite Cole, and I drop down into it.

Lucas fumbles with some keys and unlocks a drawer. Pulling out a manila folder, he walks over to us. His eyes dart between mine and Cole's, as though he's unsure he's doing the right thing.

"She doesn't know I'm aware of what's in here." I nod in understanding, and Cole sits forward, both intrigued and nervous as his leg bounces up and down.

"When I first found her, I wasn't aware she had a daughter." Hearing him say it out loud makes me wince at the thought that she has a daughter without me. With him.

My veins pump hard beneath my flesh, making me want to tear my skin off and destroy the world. For her.

"When Cole mentioned her, I couldn't understand why there was no information on them both. So, I dug deeper." He refuses to look at us, instead staring at the wall. He's struggling with his own demons of abuse too, and I have a sudden need to punish someone for their pain.

I swallow hard, knowing it's going to hurt to hear what he's about to say.

"She was reported missing from school, and when the police went to investigate, they found her chained to a radiator." He swipes a hand over his head. "Beaten." I cringe and squeeze my eyes closed. I hate him. I fucking hate him. Lucas pauses, as though composing himself to continue. He clears his throat and winces. "Naked." I feel sick to the pit of my stomach. He hurt her. Lucas shakes and squeezes his eyes closed. "Raped."

"Jesus." Cole's voice quivers, but I can't hear anything else other than the thrum of my heartbeat.

Lucas chokes on emotion and tries to mask it by clearing his throat again. "He was found passed out from alcohol, but he was arrested at the scene."

I launch to my feet, my temple pulsating. "I want him fucking dead. I want him dead. Not in jail, dead, Lucas."

Lucas's head snaps in my direction. "Sit down." His voice is cold and calculated.

When I turn to face Cole, he mirrors my expression of shock, because we both know there's more to come.

My legs wobble as I sit back down.

"They put her in protective custody."

I feel like the air is being stolen from my lungs, completely sucked from my entire soul. All this time, she didn't leave me.

She was taken from me.

My girl was unable to reach me. She was taken.

"She found out she was pregnant while in care, therefore, they took custody of Harper too."

My body shakes with shock. My poor girl. All this time I've hated her, and all this time, she was suffering. She had a baby with no one there to help her and then they took her away.

"Where the fuck is her daughter now?" I jump to my feet with a new determination in mind. Fuck Martin, I'll deal with him later. Right now, I need to fix this shit for Thalia and her little girl.

"She lives with a foster family that has been trying to adopt her."

I still at his words, my body tensing. As if sensing my unease, Cole shakes his head. "That's not what Tia wants. She's fought them every step of the way, Rage."

My shoulders loosen. Of course she has. Of course she wants her little girl. I couldn't be prouder, and yet, I feel sick at how I've treated her.

I stand firmer and puff out my chest, determined to be the man she deserves from now on. The man to protect her.

"I've been digging, and the Lancasters are very wealthy. They've . . ." Lucas pauses. " . . . been continuously difficult with Tia."

My hands ball into fists. I hate the fuckers. They took my girl's daughter and tried to bully her?

"I'm trying to do things the right way, the legal way. At the minute, our lawyer has arranged more time with Harper while he goes through the correct protocols."

"Fuck protocols!" I boom. "You get her back where she belongs, Lucas. Like, fucking now!" I stab my finger toward the floor in front of me. Thalia needs her here where she belongs.

He turns to face me, and his dark eyes meet mine. "And where does she belong, Rage?" His voice is slow and measured. I don't miss the meaning behind it.

I swallow the lump in my throat, finally able to admit to my brothers what I've been reluctant to admit. "She belongs here with us. Her family."

"Us?" He cocks a brow in question.

"Us," I repeat with confidence. "I'm all in."

Cole's eyes widen, and panic rushes inside me. "I'm not all in with you pair. Jesus, fuck no. With my girl." I cringe in disgust. "Keep your cocks away from me. I'm in for Thalia." I glance at them and hold Cole's stare. "Just Thalia," I repeat, my eyes drilling into him so he's fucking certain I don't want his dick anywhere near me.

Cole chuckles weakly.

"She has visitation tomorrow." Lucas stares at me, the intensity making my heartbeat faster. There's a question in his words, one I'm trying to figure out. "You're going to make her feel welcome, right?"

I narrow my eyes. Of course I'll make her feel welcome. What, does he think I hate kids? "Of course."

"And you'll rein in your temper?"

So, that's what he's worried about? That I'll scare her? I drag a hand through my hair. I mean, I have no experience with kids, but from my past demons, I can safely say I'd never want to scare a child. "Yes, Lucas, Jesus."

Lucas finally grants me a nod, as though I passed some test I wasn't even aware I was having. The thought annoys me, the fact he thinks he can control me pisses me the fuck off.

"Rage, chill the fuck out. He's just checking."

I look at Cole and realize I must appear angry, so I take a deep breath and step away from Lucas.

"If you feel like you're getting mad at all, just leave the room. Without smashing anything."

I flick my gaze from one of them to the other.

"Why the hell would I get mad?"

The atmosphere is icy, silent. They don't want to piss me off.

Cole clears his throat. "Her foster parents are . . ." He stops speaking as though struggling to find the words. My blood pumps rapidly through my veins.

"They're controlling," Lucas finishes for him.

"Controlling." I muse over his choice of words, dragging a shaky finger over my lip. "Do you think they hurt her?"

Cole jumps to his feet. "No. You really think I'd let Harper stay with them if I thought they hurt her?"

I swallow past the lump gathered in my throat. "No."

"Right. We wouldn't. They're just old-school."

Lucas nods in agreement. "He's right. They're an older childless couple who are a little excessive in their control. But it won't matter soon because we'll have her here with us."

"Okay." I force out my words as I accept Lucas's methods of doing things the right way.

"So, where are we taking her tomorrow?" Cole's eyes light up when he speaks, and a ripple of jealousy runs through me that they have gotten to meet her, and I haven't. They already have a relationship with her, and I don't.

"Maybe the zoo?" Lucas suggests.

I turn on my heel, ignoring their discussions about kid-friendly places before I explode in a jealous fit of rage and storm back into the bedroom.

As soon as her scent encompasses me, I relax. Her beautiful blue eyes find mine from over the top of the sheets, and she gifts me with a sad smile, one that makes me want to make everything right for her. Be a better person for her.

"Hey."

"Hey." I smile back.

Thalia sits up. "Should we talk?"

I shake my head as I walk toward the bed, because the last thing I want to do is talk to her right now.

Right now, I need to show her how much she means to me.

"I'd rather we didn't." I lift my shirt over my head and drop it to the floor.

"Please?" Her nervous voice slices into me, and her

eyes lower. Shit, I need to do this. Be the man she deserves me to be, not the one just filled with rage.

I drag a hand over my messy hair. "Sure, baby, whatever you need."

Her shoulders sag in relief, reminding me of how big of an ass I was for not wanting to discuss feelings.

She lifts the sheet for me to climb in beside her, and I lie with my arm rested behind my head and tug her toward me. Her small hand rests on my stomach, and even that innocent gesture makes my cock twitch.

"I should have been there for you, Thalia. It fucking guts me that I wasn't." The stab in my heart makes my fists tense in defense. I let her down. I left her to that sick fucker, and when Lucas figures shit out, I'm going to take great delight in punishing him.

Thalia feels the shift in me because she tenses. "It wasn't on you, Jace. You couldn't have known what he was capable of."

She's wrong. I knew what he was capable of; I knew he was evil. I just never realized he'd go as far as he did or touch her sexually. I was naïve, a naïve kid who was living in a dream world about creating a perfect life and rescuing her from the bad. I just never realized how bad it was for her. Or maybe I just refused to see the bigger picture? The thought that I could have dug deeper or seen more signs sends a wave of sickness through my body and makes my throat incredibly dry.

"Tell me about her," I implore, desperate to change the subject. I'm a coward, I know it, but I'm well aware that unless I have somewhere to release my growing rage with thoughts of Martin, I'm not going to be able to give her this softer side of me.

Thalia smiles against my chest. "She's so cute, Jace, and clever too. She's good at art like me. She loves animals."

This piques my interest because my brothers mentioned a zoo for her visitation. "What animal does she like best?"

"Giraffes, one hundred percent." Thalia laughs against me. "She had a stuffed giraffe toy when she was a baby, and she still has it now."

Threading my fingers through Thalia's, I imagine her with a baby. My breath hitches at the thought that I've missed that. Something else Martin stole from me.

I roll her onto her back so I can properly survey her body. I gently trail my fingers over her tits, pushing them together, then circling her much bigger nipples—probably from motherhood. My tongue darts out of my mouth to taste them, but I continue my descent, only now noticing the vague white lines on her stomach, giving away what would have been for accommodating her little girl. Gently, I place a kiss on them, and Thalia gasps at the touch of my lips. I trace my fingers over her pussy and down to her hole. Without warning, I thrust two fingers inside. My cock jumps at the wetness surrounding my fingers, eager to get in on the action.

"Your body has changed so much, Thalia, but your pussy is still nice and tight, baby."

She clenches around my fingers as I pump them faster.

"Please, Jace. I need you."

I slip my fingers out of her and push down my joggers. Positioning myself above her, my lips graze hers, and our eyes connect.

"I love you, Thalia."

"I love you too. I never stopped."

And with that, I push inside her, determined to make her forget.

I'm going to spend the rest of the day showing her just how much she means to me, and the past can stay where it is for now.

In the past.

CHAPTER
THIRTEEN

Tia

Jace has been attached to me since yesterday. He even went as far as sitting in the back of the SUV with me so he can hold my hand. His hand feels clammy, and he keeps chewing the inside of his mouth, giving away he's anxious about meeting Harper. I want nothing more than to protect him from those feelings.

I turn to face him, slowly trailing my hand over his jawline. "Hey, it's fine."

His eyes lock with mine, and his Adam's apple bobs. "I just want her to like me."

My heart soars at his words.

I was scared of Jace blaming Harper for her conception. I thought his hate would cloud his judgment, but now, staring into his dark eyes, I know, without a shadow of a doubt, this man just wants to be loved by

111

my little girl, and it's then I fall deeper in love with him, something I thought was impossible until now.

"She'll love you, Jace."

"You think?" He searches my face for a trace of uncertainty. "You said she likes giraffes, right?"

I bite into my lip with a nod.

"Good." The one-word answer leaves me confused, but I have no time to analyze it because the SUV pulls to a stop.

"Lucas is over there." Cole points toward the gates to the zoo, and my pulse races with excitement as I try to get out of the car and join them. I fumble to open the door, and before my feet touch the ground, I hear her squeal in delight.

"Mommy!"

She runs toward me, and I meet her halfway, bending down to greet her. Harper's hands wrap around my neck.

"I missed you." I breathe into her hair as I squeeze her tightly.

"I missed you too, Mommy." She pulls back to look at me. "Lucas says there are giraffes and crocodiles in the zoo, can we go see?"

Jace shadows me, and I stand. "Harper, this is Mommy's friend, Jace. Can you say hi?"

Harper scrunches up her nose, scrutinizing Jace, who kneels down so he's level with her.

I can see the nervousness rolling off him, the shake of his hand when he holds it out for Harper. "Nice to meet you, Harper."

"You have pictures on you." She ignores his hand and instead points to his neck.

Jace chuckles awkwardly and withdraws his hand. "Yeah, they're tattoos."

"I like 'em." She grins at him.

"You do?" Shock mars his face, and I melt at the look of relief on him.

"Yeah. Can I choose one for you to paint on you?" Harper asks.

"Sure." Jace chuckles back at Harper happily. The moment between them feels like a dream. I never thought I'd see him again, let alone with my daughter.

Cole's hand bands around my waist and tugs me gently toward him. "I missed you, beauty." He nuzzles into my neck, sending a surge of arousal through me.

My eyes drift to Lucas; he's watching us with heavy eyes, and I fidget under his scrutiny.

"Harper wants to go see the crocodiles, are you guys joining us?" Jace chuckles playfully as he tugs Harper into his arms. Her little fingers trace over the tattoos on his neck.

I snap out of my thoughts and pull away from Cole, who groans at my movement. I don't miss him adjusting himself as my hand falls into Jace's and we head toward the reptile enclosure.

LUCAS

I watch Tia throughout the day. Rage is glued to her and Harper's sides with Cole following behind like a lapdog, and I'm well aware I'm here as a spare part, and I fucking hate it.

Sure, she keeps smiling over me with a look of sympathy in her eyes, but I don't want her sympathy. I want her to want me like I want her. I want her devotion.

My love for her is brutal and all-consuming, but I hide it as best as I can behind a mask of indifference. I smile on cue and smirk at Cole's awkward jokes.

He sees me, though; he sees the pain hidden behind my feigned expressions.

I want to punish her for it, punish her for making me feel pushed out, simply forgotten.

"You look like you're about to whip her ass." Cole smirks as he straddles the bench overlooking the sea lion viewing area.

Harper's shrill squeal draws our attention as Rage

takes out his phone and snaps a shot of Tia and Harper feeding the sea lions.

"She loves us." His voice is low and edged with anxiety.

I nod but remain silent, because right now, my thoughts would tip Cole over the edge.

Am I insane to think that this could work between us?

They look like the perfect family together, and we're sitting here on the outside looking in. My heart freefalls, making it difficult for me to breathe.

"It's okay, man." He strokes his palm over my shoulder in a way that I'd normally despise, but today? Today, I need him, and I accept his touch willingly.

Tia turns her head over her shoulder to search for us, and her hair floats around her, making her look like an angel. Her face softens, and she says something to Jace, then strides toward us. My heart hammers as I take in every curve of her body, every sway of her hips.

"Are you both okay?" Her soft voice sends a flutter to my stomach, and I will myself to reach out and touch her. But I've never had a physical relationship before, let alone in public.

As if sensing my thoughts, she lowers herself onto my lap and bands an arm around my neck. "I missed you." My chest tightens at her admission. "I'm with you tonight, right?" My grip tightens on her thighs, and when she wiggles her ass, my cock thickens in my pants.

"Tia," I growl out in warning.

She brings her lips to my neck and drags her tongue

116

toward my ear. "Please say you'll fuck me. Please, Daddy."

I close my eyes at her words.

Fucking Jesus.

"Fuck me, that's hot." Cole strokes his hand over his jean-clad cock, and my eyes dart around the zoo to make sure nobody is watching.

"Mmm, Cole is hard for us, Daddy." She grinds her ass down on me, her breath tickling my neck.

"Tia. You're being bad right now."

"Mmm, so bad."

My cock leaks at her filthy mouth, and a groan slips from my tight jaw. My cock is nestled tightly between her ass cheeks, giving me the perfect amount of friction.

My hands grip her thighs so tight I'm sure they'll leave a mark, but I'm beyond caring. I push her hair aside, exposing the mark that Rage widened on her neck. He thought it would piss me off, rile me.

But all it did was make me hard imagining them together, with him completely obsessed and devoted to her.

I tenderly kiss the mark and relish in the shudder that takes over her body. Knowing she wants me as much as I want her is the comfort I need right now and she knows it.

She grinds down again on my cock, and my body tightens.

"Daddy." She pants in my ear, causing my hips to move up against her ass.

"Fuck, beauty. Make him come. Make him come right

117

here in the open." Cole stares at us with lust-filled eyes, his cock bulging in his jeans. It makes me wish I could see his desperation.

"Mmm, I want you to come." Her bratty voice sends a tremor down my spine and a tingle to my balls.

"Fuck. Grind on Daddy's lap, baby girl," I pant out.

She pushes down harder.

"Make Daddy come." I nip at her neck, and she throws her head back to expose her throat. With a tight hand around her throat, I push her down on my cock.

"Take Daddy."

Her mouth drops open. "Yes, Daddy."

My cock pulsates, sending cum spurting into my pants. "Fuck, yes." I lift my hips into her ass, thrust after thrust.

I slowly come down from my orgasm to find Cole wide-eyed and open mouthed.

"Are your panties wet?"

Tia swallows before answering, "Yes."

"Are you close to coming?" My voice is still rugged.

"Yes."

"Good girl," I coo as my hand gently strokes over her body. "Come on, let's go to the SUV." I pull her up to me and fire a text off to Rage to inform him to amuse Harper for the next twenty minutes. "We need to be quick."

COLE

We climb into the back of the SUV.

As soon as the door slams shut, I unbuckle my belt and pop open my jeans.

Watching Lucas come in his pants was something else. The look of euphoria on his face made me nearly bust in my pants.

My brother has never so much as kissed a woman in public, so to come was a huge milestone, and I felt a part of it. It was amazing.

I pull out my dripping cock. Running a finger over my piercing makes me fuck my hand harder.

Tia pulls down her leggings, exposing a G-string that I quickly snap in two while Lucas takes out his cum-covered cock. I lick my lips in awe when Tia drags her tongue down his shaft without needing instruction. He tilts his head back against the headrest on a moan.

"Fuck her, brother. Fuck Daddy's little girl real good."

Lucas doesn't so much as lift his head, as though he's so completely turned on, he's in a trance.

"Fuck, lick your Daddy's cock clean, beauty."

She moans around his cock, and I can only imagine what the vibrations must be doing to him, because his fist tightens in her hair. I position myself behind her, which is fucking hard in an SUV. I have one foot on the floor, and my other leg is bent on the seat. I surge forward, her warm pussy encompasses my cock, and I groan when my piercing hits deep.

Tia splutters around Lucas with the force of my thrust. "Fuck, beauty. I'll never get enough of this pussy, you hear me? Never."

Lucas stares down at her, his eyelids heavy. "Choke on my cock, baby girl." He holds her head down as I hammer into her from behind.

My eyes latch on to her tight asshole, and without any preparation, I push my thumb through the tight muscle, making her clench around my cock and gurgle all the more on Lucas.

"Fuck, yes. She likes a thumb in her ass, brother."

His eyes flit to the motion of me fucking her ass with my thumb while I fuck her pussy hard.

"Jesus." Lucas's voice drops an octave.

"Come, baby girl. Come for Daddy with my brother fucking you good."

My head drops forward as Tia's pussy squeezes my cock with such force I see stars.

I sense the minute Lucas comes too; a rumble expels

from his panting chest as Tia's spine arches into my touch. We all come together.

Brutally together.

CHAPTER

FOURTEEN

J ace

I can't take my eyes off her. She's everything.

At first, I was worried I'd look at her and see him. See the man I hate with every fiber of my being.

But all I see is Thalia and the sweet little girl I knew. She's the mirror image of her mom, and I love it. I love her. How's it possible to know of a child for less than twenty-four hours and yet fall utterly and completely into devoted love with them?

"And Miss Sharpe said I can move up a level in math because I'm so good at it."

I grin over at Harper; she hasn't shut up talking about school for the past half an hour. "Your mom wasn't very good at math."

"Oh, I know. She once said she knew a boy that was so clever at math, he got to go to a university on a sc . . . a sc . . ." She presses her finger to her lip, deep in thought.

"A scholarship?" I suggest. A dull ache tugs deep inside me at the thought of Thalia mentioning me to her daughter.

"Yes, one of those!" She grins triumphantly back at me, and I can't help but mirror her reaction.

"Do you want to go feed the giraffes?"

"We can?" Her eyes light up in excitement.

"I booked us a spot so you can go in and feed them from your hands."

"No way!" She sucks in a sharp breath that makes me chuckle. "Yes please, Jace!"

"Great, come on, Little T. Let's go."

She smiles at me so wide her whole face lights up, and I revel in the fact I put her smile there.

AFTER MEETING BACK UP with Thalia and my brothers, we went for dinner followed by some more animals and a trip to the gift store, which ended with us all buying Harper a stuffed toy. Thalia rolled her eyes and giggled at the antics between us because Harper did not want the biggest ones on the shelf. Nope, she wanted the little ones, and here's me thinking bigger is always better.

"She'll want to hide them in her backpack," Lucas grunts low while Cole and Thalia take Harper toward the restrooms to go change.

His words irk me. "I want her living with us. Where she belongs." Where I can protect her, but I don't mention that part. An overwhelming urge to protect her when I failed her mom consumes me.

"I'm working on it," he spits the words out at me as though pissed.

"Work fucking harder," I snap back. "Hiding her fucking soft toys?" I stare at him, as though he's crazed. Why the hell would she have to hide soft toys?

He shrugs a shoulder. "I told you. They're old-school."

I scoff at him in disgust; they must be fucking ancient not to accept soft toys.

We walk out the store toward the parking lot, meeting a distraught Harper and a teary-eyed Thalia.

"What the fuck happened?" I snap. My temple pulsates, and my hands ball into fists with the need to tear apart whoever hurt my girls.

Cole is kneeling beside Harper, trying to comfort her, and I refrain from ripping him away from her and pulling her into my arms.

"She's sad she has to go back to the Lancasters'," Thalia explains on a sniffle. "I can't bring myself to say, 'Take her home,' because that isn't her home. Her home is with me, wherever I am. That's her home." Thalia raises her chin in defiance, and I nod in pride at my girl. Damn right, she's her home. We all are.

"I just want to stay with you." Harper hiccups between sobs.

"I know, peanut. We're working really hard to make that happen," Thalia says in a soothing voice, brushing Harper's hair from her face.

"But I like being with you and the boys."

I can't help but smile when she calls us boys.

"I know, sweetheart, but Mommy needs you to be brave just a little longer, okay?"

Harper sniffles. "I'll try."

"Good job, sweetie. Now, give Mommy hugs, and Lucas is going to take you back to the Lancasters' house, okay?"

I turn to Lucas for an explanation.

"Thalia struggles leaving her, and the Lancasters are less than inviting, so I offered."

I nod in approval at my brother protecting her.

Cole takes Harper by the hand and proceeds to strap her into her car seat while Thalia kisses her cheek.

I step up to the little girl who has stolen my heart.

"Penguin?" she smiles.

I hold my nose close to hers, then she brushes it against my own, making her giggle. "Goodbye, Jace. I'll see you soon."

"Yeah, you will, Little T."

Real fucking soon.

STEPPING into the back of the SUV, I automatically tug Thalia close to me, needing her as much as she needs me. I seek comfort in her, and I know she needs it too. It's been a big day. A day I never imagined possible nor let myself envisage.

As we pull away from the parking lot, I stroke down

Thalia's arm, a need to protect her so strong, it makes my muscles lock tight.

I breathe through my nose to try and calm myself, but the air is thick with something.

I glance around the vehicle as though the answers are going to jump out at me. "Why the fuck does the car smell like sex?"

Thalia chokes on a playful silent sob while Cole grins from ear to ear through the rearview mirror.

"We fucked Tia while you were feeding the monkeys."

"They were fucking giraffes, dipshit."

Cole shrugs. "What the fuck ever. I was feeding a pussy."

Thalia lets out a giggle at our banter, and just like that, the cloud of solemness is lifted.

I stare down at my girl nestled under my arm, and for the first time since learning of her relationship with my brothers, I'm not jealous.

I'm actually pretty fucking grateful she has them too.

CHAPTER
FIFTEEN

Lucas

I flick the camera app down and watch Tia sashay toward my office in my work shirt with an obvious purpose in mind. Me.

As soon as she steps into my office, my cock swells. I lean back in my chair and widen my legs to make room for it.

"You said we would be together tonight." Her sultry voice sends a wave of arousal through my body, and when she nibbles her bottom lip, I can't help the groan that catches in my throat.

"I did."

Tia slowly unbuttons the shirt she's wearing, and while she's doing so, I unbuckle my pants. Pushing down the waistband on my boxers, I tuck them under my balls.

Slowly, I stroke my cock up and down. My gaze takes in her delectable body inch by fucking inch. Her breasts are heavy and her nipples are peaked, making my mouth water to latch on to them.

I imagine her pregnant with our child, her stomach round and her breasts swollen, and my cock jumps at the thought. Sticky pre-cum drips from the tip, so I rub my thumb over the slit with one hand while I motion for her to kneel between my legs with the other.

Completely naked and bare to me, Tia kneels.

"Suck my thumb, baby girl." I gift her with my pre-cum-soaked thumb, and she sticks out her little tongue in anticipation, drawing my thumb into her mouth, eliciting a hiss from me. "You suck like such a good girl." Her tongue wraps around my thumb, and she moans on a whimper when she sucks harder, making my fist tighten on my cock.

Languorously, I withdraw my thumb with a pop.

"Undress me." My voice is choked and full of need, and given the way the flush creeps over her cheeks, my commands are affecting her as much as me.

She rushes to help undress me, and I help by kicking off my shoes and socks. She tugs down my pants and boxers when I lift my ass for her, then works quickly to unbutton my shirt.

Not so long ago, I was terrified of anyone touching me, but now? Now, I relish in her touch.

I glance at the computer and make a note of the time, knowing exactly when Cole is due home.

She pushes my shirt off my shoulders, and I can't help the groan that escapes me. "Fuck me, you're beautiful. Now, climb on Daddy's lap and push those tits in my face like a good baby girl."

"Mmm, does Daddy like?"

I smirk at her, knowing how much she likes the games we play—just as much as me. I take hold of one of her tits and tug it toward my waiting mouth, closing my eyes with the soft sensation of her skin against my tongue and her nipple pebbling under each flick.

Tia's nails dig into my shoulders as she straddles me. Rubbing her pussy over my cock, she moans into my neck.

Her lips find the flesh below my ear, and she nips at me, making me grind my hips against her.

I pop off her nipple. "Be a good girl and spin around to face the door."

She moves without hesitation; her compliance makes my cock eager to reward her.

Tia wraps her legs over mine so I'm opening her up nice and wide.

Gently, I trail my finger down her spine. I stop when I reach the carved marks of our joint ownership on her body. Slowly, I graze a finger over them, then I lift her hips and move my cock to position at her hole. Wetness is gathered, making it easy for me to slide in, gently lowering her all the way to the hilt.

"Ahh, Daddy." She winces at the stretch of her pussy, and the darkness inside me relishes in it.

"Be a good fucking girl and take all Daddy's cock." I clench my teeth to ward off the need to slam into her.

Bending her slightly forward with one hand on her

hip and the other bracing around her lithe body, I roll her nipple between my fingers, eliciting another moan from her greedy lips.

My body is coiled tight beneath her, desperate to unleash the beast, but also desperate for *him* to witness it too.

She wiggles from side to side, and I allow her to. My gaze darts up from the marks on her lower back toward the door as a wide-eyed Cole steps into the room.

"Holy fuuuuck." He scrubs a disbelieving hand down his face, and that's when I unleash, determined to give him a show.

I move my hand from her tit and instead take her hair and wrap it around my fist. Aggressively slamming her back against my chest, I drive into her, thrust after fucking thrust.

I'm vaguely aware of Cole undressing as I continue my assault on her pussy.

"Oh god. Oh god, Lucas." She wraps her arms around my neck, stretching her whole body out in front of Cole so he can see every inch of me taking her from behind.

His naked body stands between my legs, and I can't help but stare at his fist swiftly pumping his cock. He's so close to us, yet so far, and I can't figure out how to tell him I want more, because truthfully, I don't know what more is.

"Fuck me. I want to lick your pussy so bad right now, Tia." Cole's Adam's apple bobs, and the thought of him tasting her while I'm inside her sends a spurt of cum from my cock and forces my eyes to close.

"Please."

I open my eyes on her words to see her staring at me, asking for permission for Cole to lick her while I'm deep inside her. Fuck me, that's hot.

My chest tightens. Can I do that? Can I feel him between my legs like that? I lick my suddenly dry lips and force past the lump in my throat, turning my head to face Cole once again. "Get on your knees and lick her pussy, brother."

Cole's eyes flare with both shock and arousal before he quickly drops to his knees. His thick hands landing on my thighs makes me wince and squirm with delight all in one go.

His hot breath consumes me, and I can't help the groan and thrust of my hips when the force of his face presses against Tia, therefore pushing her further against me.

With every slurping noise Cole makes, I imagine him latching on to her clit and flicking his tongue over the swollen bud of nerves. Tia releases a moan that hits me straight in the balls and makes her pussy clench uncontrollably tight around me, making me struggle to force down every cell in my body that tells me I'm going to come.

"Fuck, Tia, you taste so good with my brother's cock inside you," Cole pants.

Realizing one hand is no longer on my thigh, annoyance bubbles inside me. I never gave him permission to touch himself.

"Are you fucking your hand, Cole?" I snap out,

annoyed that he might be getting off on just her pussy when I'm struggling because of them both.

His grip tightens on my thighs as he sits kneeling between my legs, staring at Tia's pussy in complete awe while I slowly drag my cock in and out of her, putting on a show for him.

"Fuck, brother. If I touch myself, I'll come. Jesus, I need to taste you both." His admission makes my heart soar.

"Please." Tia stares up at me, her blue eyes shimmering with desperation. "Please, let him taste us both." She releases a hand from around my neck, places a tender kiss on my jaw, then turns her attention to Cole. "I need him to lick me, Daddy." Her hand finds her clit, and I watch in amazement as she circles her clit for us.

My heart pounds as I take in Cole, who remains stoically still, staring at me, waiting for my command, and the thought of control makes my need for them become undeniable.

"Lick my cock too."

His mouth drops open in shock. Then, he quickly moves, as though worried I'll change my mind.

He drags his tongue over the base of my cock, and the vibration of a groan from him makes my balls draw up. My muscles tense, and Tia whimpers in need as I imagine he's reached her clit, then he repeats the motion. My body is tense with satisfaction, the urge to come almost overwhelming as his warm tongue and piercing flicks over my cock and around my balls. "Jesus, Cole."

I can feel a mixture of his dribble and her arousal flood my balls, and I work myself slowly in and out, the tortuous feeling like no other.

"Oh god. Cole." Her hand finds his head and mine finds her hand as we both hold his head in place. My hips begin to pump faster and faster at the thought of fucking his face while Tia thrusts her hips into him too. We're a tangled, filthy mess, and it feels sensational.

"Lick my balls, brother. Fuck, lick my balls."

His warm tongue laps around my balls, and I don't know how much more I can take. My toes curl and my body tenses.

"Oh god, Daddy. Daddy, I'm going to . . ." Tia screams out her release as my cock expands. My mouth falls open on a loud grunt while Cole jumps to his feet and quickly jerks his cock over us. His warm cum shoots over my balls and covers Tia's pussy, her hand moves between her legs, and she coats us with his cum, making my head drop back in satisfaction.

Our chests heave in unison as a coldness takes over me with the realization of what I've just done. I have another man's cum on me when I promised myself never again.

My body freezes, and my eyes dart to Cole who watches me with anxiety.

Tia's hand finds my cheek, and she turns me to face her. Her eyes beg, *Please don't ruin it*, and I swallow past the need to run.

"I'm gonna go jump in the shower." Cole turns

quickly, a look of uncertainty in his eyes, and I hate myself for putting it there.

As soon as the door closes, Tia moves from my lap, and my cum drips out of her pussy and down her thighs. I find it mesmerizing.

"Good thing I'm on birth control, huh?" She grins down at her legs, making me wince at the knowledge I'm withholding.

SIXTEEN

Rage
I slam my fist into the bag again, imagining I'm pummeling that sick prick's face. The need for vengeance against him is festering inside me.

The bag sways with each blow, and sweat pours from my body. It's been a week since we saw Harper, and we've gotten into a steady routine of taking it in turns to have Thalia for the night. Tonight, it's my turn, and the thought of being with her is the only thing stopping me from going over to the Lancasters' and stealing Harper away.

"Are you sure you don't want to fight on Saturday?" Trent, one of our trainers, asks with a quirk of his brow.

I jump in the air, delivering the perfect roundhouse kick to the bag. "Nope."

After seeing the tortured expression on Thalia's face when she saw me all busted up, I'm not in a rush to see it again. I want to make my woman happy, and the need to protect her from everything—including myself—is my main priority right now. Besides, once this shit is taken care of, I'm hoping my rage simmers down.

My phone vibrates on the gym bench, and I stroll over to it, taking a drink from my water bottle. I spit it out when I see the image on the screen.

Holy fucking hell.

Thalia is laid out with her legs open and has cum dripping from her pussy.

I quickly glance around the gym like an idiot to make sure no one can see my girl begging for more cum. My cock aches at the sight.

> Lucas: She's ready and waiting. Are you coming back soon, or are we having another round here while you have another round there?

My chest tightens with anger. They're fucking her right now? On my day?!

I swipe my gym bag from the floor and storm out the door.

GIGGLES FILL my ears as I enter the apartment, but I refuse to acknowledge the happiness around them. Instead, I storm into Cole's bedroom, slamming the door behind me.

I stab at my chest. "It was my fucking day." I'm aware

I sound like a petulant child, but I can't help myself.

Lucas leans back in the armchair, ever the voyeur, while Cole is lying on his bed naked. Stroking his cock, he kisses Thalia and ignores me completely. Her eyes dart to mine, but he pulls her face away and instead forces a kiss on her that I feel all the way in my balls.

"Fuck." I pull my shirt over my head and drop my shorts, allowing my thick cock to spring against my stomach.

I move toward the bed, take hold of her ankles, and throw her unexpectedly onto her stomach, forcing her and Cole apart.

"Get on your fucking knees, Thalia. Can't even wait for my goddamn cock before you need filling?" I slap her ass hard, leaving a mark. It's then my eyes latch on to the engraving just above her ass. What. The. Actual. Fuck?

My eyes bug out. Then, as quickly as the shock arrives, jealousy consumes me. Because their names are on her and not mine. She's marked as theirs but not mine. My anger flares, rage transcends through to my fingers, my hand rises, and I smack her hard, already leaving behind a red mark. "Fucking whore!" I spit the words out, meaning every goddamn word of it right now.

She turns her head over her shoulders. "I'm Daddy's little whore." She smirks toward Lucas, and my eyebrows shoot up, because, what the fuck?

My head spins toward him. Just what the hell has been going on between them? And what the hell am I missing out on? My cock sure as hell likes the thought of it.

Lucas smirks back at me, then strokes his cock lazily. The fact that I'm in my brother's room with their cocks out doesn't faze me. Right now, it just feels right.

"Give me your fucking knife!"

Lucas scans over my face.

"Now, Lucas!"

He fumbles with the heap of clothes at his feet and quickly locates his knife, handing it to me with a stern look that tells me not to fuck this up.

I flick open the blade, and the sound makes my cock jump. "Hold her fucking arms," I snap in Cole's direction. He moves in front of Thalia and takes a hold of her arms so she can't pull away.

Slowly, I drag the tip of the blade above Lucas's name. I'm her first fucking love, so I deserve to be at the top. I dig the tip into her flesh, relishing in the hiss of her breath and the flinch of her body beneath it.

Blood oozes from the wound as I dig a little deeper to make sure I last longer than their names.

Thalia's body shakes slightly, and I caress her skin to reassure her. When the last letter is complete, I stare down in sick fascination at the masterpiece before me.

Jace.

Lucas.

Cole.

Devoted.

My eyes trail over the perfect curve of her back, the toned globes of her ass, and her tight little asshole. I lick my lips as the blood seeps into the crack of her ass.

"She's never been fucked in the ass, brother. We

saved that for you." My eyes snap up to Lucas, who is staring at me with a daring, truthful expression.

My cock leaks with excitement, and I have an overwhelming urge to take her virginity there too.

I lean over her and spit on her ass as the blood and spittle mix together to create the perfect lubricant. I drag the tip of my cock to her hole, lathering it with the perfect pinkened mixture of us both as I push gently into her muscled barrier.

"Ohh." She whimpers and tenses below me. Annoyance rumbles inside me at her discomfort. I want to both punish her and cherish her.

"Feed her your cock, brother," Lucas suggests to Cole, but he doesn't move, making me force eye contact with him. He stares back at me, as though waiting for my approval. I nod back at him before flicking my gaze back down to my hand currently feeding my thick cock into her tiny asshole.

"Fuck, baby. You're doing so damn good. Your hole is so small for me." I push further in, another inch, another clench of my teeth, as she stretches around me.

"Oh." She whimpers around Cole's cock.

I move to rub circles on her clit. The motion makes her relax and gurgle around Cole's cock. His eyes are completely transfixed on him lazily fucking her face.

I never intended to share her like this with my brothers, and it's not something I'm going to make a habit of because I love our alone time. Just us.

But right now, with my cock pushed all the way inside her ass, swimming in our juices and Cole's pants of approval along with the slapping of Lucas's fist against his cock, I can see me making an occasional exception.

I pull out, then slam back in. Cole holds her in position as I repeat the motion, my balls already feeling heavy with the need to empty inside her.

"Fuck, I need her mouth. Fuck, I need to come in her mouth." Lucas pants, completely unraveling.

I nod toward Cole, who's still engrossed in Thalia's blowjob skills.

Lucas pushes Cole out of the way and quickly feeds Thalia his cock. Her mouth drips with spittle as she works from one cock to the other, and I close my eyes, determined not to come yet.

"Fuck, give Daddy that mouth. Take us. Take us both, baby girl."

I watch, completely and utterly consumed with arousal, as they both push their cocks into Thalia's greedy mouth.

"Oh fuck, that's good. Oh fuck," Cole chants, his whole chest heaving. His body tenses as he grips Thalia's hair.

Lucas's mouth drops open silently, and his body wobbles as he comes too, flooding her stuffed mouth.

"Fuuuuuck!" I come on a roar, and my head drops forward as ropes upon ropes of cum shoot out my cock while Thalia clenches tighter around me, letting me know she's coming too.

"I love you so damn much, Thalia."

Tia

I startle awake at the sound of my phone vibrating. Checking the clock beside the bed, I groan when I realize it's just after 7:00 a.m.

I quickly glance at the boys. Cole is one side of me, and Lucas is on the other while Jace is sleeping with his head on my stomach with his body curled in half. I drag my fingers through his hair again and reach for my phone.

My heart sinks when I see it's Mrs. Lancaster calling, no doubt to rearrange Harper's visitation.

I clear my throat and try to sound put together, mature. "Hello, Mrs. Lancaster, is everything okay?"

"No. No it's not. Harper has been involved in a road traffic collision. She's currently at Jefferson Memorial."

My world stands still, and my mind goes blank.

I'm not sure what's happening around me, but all I see are the boys up and pulling on their clothes. Then,

Cole pushes my hands through a T-shirt while Lucas guides me to stand.

"It's okay, baby." Jace tugs me into him.

"We're here for you, beauty." Cole kisses my forehead as we move out of the bedroom. Somehow, I get into the SUV and we make our way toward the hospital.

LUCAS

I felt the change in her as soon as she answered the incessant buzzing noise. I knew—*I knew*—something had happened to Harper because nothing else could possibly cause that reaction.

When I took the phone from her, the Lancaster bitch tried to tell me it wasn't necessary for Tia to come to the hospital. Wouldn't that be the perfect ammunition for the courts? That her own mother didn't attend the hospital?

Rage strides ahead. Swinging open the double doors, he barks orders at the receptionist, and before we even reach the desk, he knows where to locate Harper.

Tia clings to Cole like he's her lifeline, and I guess out of the three of us, he's certainly the one most in touch with his feelings and the most levelheaded.

We stride toward the intensive care unit, and my stomach drops, realizing the severity of the situation.

Rage is greeted by a doctor who shakes his hand, and

he then motions toward a room. We all walk inside, and for the first time, she breaks away from Cole to stand beside Rage. Cole stands behind her with his hand on her hip while I dig my hand in my pocket to stroke over my knife for comfort.

"She's currently been placed in a coma to give her body time to regain control. Unfortunately, the impact of the vehicle left her with internal bleeding to her stomach, and during the surgery, she lost a lot of blood. We may need to give her another blood transfusion."

I wince at the explanation given by the doctor.

"You're welcome to go in and sit with her, but please know the machines and tubes are for Harper's benefit." He stares sympathetically toward Tia.

Tia, Rage, and Cole push through the door while I hang back to speak to the doctor.

"What actually happened?"

The doctor clears his throat and looks toward the door. "Mrs. Lancaster said she ran across the road and was struck by an oncoming vehicle. A witness at the scene said they saw a scuffle between Harper and Mrs. Lancaster, and Harper ran away."

"A scuffle?" I question.

"The police are currently investigating." He gives me a curt nod.

My chest feels like it's collapsing. Did I completely misjudge the situation? Did leaving Harper in their care while I did things the legal way put her in harm's way?

I suck in a sharp breath, gasping for air. Did I hurt her?

"Sir!" The doctor clears his throat. "She's in good hands. What's important right now is getting Harper better."

My head rises to meet his concerned expression.

I give him a sharp nod and push past him into the room, determined to get to the bottom of the Lancasters once and for all.

CHAPTER
EIGHTEEN

Tia

When Jace pushed open the doors to Harper's room, I felt like my life had come to an end. My beautiful bubbly little girl was barely visible among countless tubes, wires, and machines. Her pale, lifeless body made my head float and my legs give way.

I've never felt pain like it, and knowing there's nothing I can do to help her is nothing short of soul destroying.

I lift my head from her bed. I'm not sure how many hours we've been here or where the Lancasters are, but right now, I'm grateful for their absence because I just want my little girl. Just me and her, how it should be.

Jace sits beside me stroking my hair while Cole and Lucas are in a heated chatter, but I'm beyond caring. I just want my little girl back.

I stare down at our entwined fingers, willing for a

flicker of life to come from hers. For even the tiniest of grip so I know she's still there. Still fighting.

Guilt floods me. I should have done more. I should have fought harder. I should have been the mom she deserves. A sob catches in my throat.

Jace pulls me into his lap as I tighten my balled hand into his shirt and cry while he rocks me. "Shh, baby, it's going to be okay."

"It's not. I'm not good enough for her. I'm not good enough. She deserves better."

His spine snaps straight, and he pulls me back to stare into his eyes. His hands hold my cheeks in place as he brings his forehead to mine. "You're good enough, Thalia. You're her everything, and when she wakes up, it's you she'll want. You hear me?" Tears stream down my face, and my heart races. "Tell me who she'll ask for when she wakes up, Thalia." His stern words drill into me, leaving me no choice but to answer truthfully.

"Me. She'll ask for me."

His shoulders relax. "That's right, baby. She'll ask for you."

I nod in agreement, knowing he's right.

The door opens, and the doctor who we spoke to earlier walks in, his face a picture of concern. He holds his hand up when I jump from Jace's lap and rush toward him. "Please, I don't want you to worry, this is just precautionary." Cole steps behind me and places his hand on my shoulder for comfort. "We've decided to get donations of blood in case Harper needs another transfusion. We look to the biological parents, first and foremost."

My heart beats faster at his words, and panic races through me. I can't breathe. Oh my god, I can't breathe.

"You can give blood, Tia." Lucas's words slice through my heart, making me wish that were true.

I shake my head and grip my hair in a complete panic. "I . . . I can't." I dart my gaze around the room, but the confused expressions on their faces only add to my unraveling panic. "I can't. I'm not a match. I'm not a match!" I scream at the top of my lungs.

Cole pulls me into his chest and grips me tight, his chest heaving with emotion.

"He doesn't know about her." I struggle to get my words out between tortured sobs. "He doesn't know." I tilt my head to Cole. "Please don't make them tell him. Please," I beg. "Please."

He swallows thickly. "I won't, beauty."

"Cole," Lucas snaps in warning.

"Shut the fuck up. There has to be another way. He's not going anywhere near them. I'll give fucking blood." He stares at Lucas with conviction.

The doctor steps forward. "Harper has a rare blood type."

I squeeze my eyes closed, refusing to accept his words.

Jace licks his lips. "What blood type is she?"

"She's AB negative." The doctor confirms what I already know.

Jace smiles to himself. "Well, fuck me. That's the same type as mine."

I stare at him in confusion, because he can't be joking right now, right? "What?"

"Are you sure?" Lucas asks.

Jace snorts. "The number of times docs have patched me up, I'm telling you I know my blood type." He smirks with confidence.

The doctor turns to face him. "That's a one percent chance. Extremely rare, something we only see in biological families."

"Tia. What are the chances that Jace could be Harper's father?" Lucas stares at me in shock.

My heart skips a beat, and Jace's face turns deathly pale. "I . . . we . . . we used protection."

Lucas nods but doesn't say a word.

I bite into my lip when a wave of sickness encompasses me at the thought of my next words. "He . . . he didn't." I close my eyes at the pain.

As if understanding, the doctor nods. "I'll arrange blood tests for you both. Just to be on the safe side." He writes on his clipboard and leaves the room.

Jace stares wistfully back toward the bed. "You think she could be mine?"

My lips answer truthfully.

"I don't know."

CHAPTER NINETEEN

C ole

Anger surges through me, and I feel the need to drive my fist into someone's face, or at the very least, a wall. She's hurting beyond anything that we could ever know, and I hate the fact there's not a damn thing we can do to help.

When Rage declared he's a match for Harper, elation and relief entered my heart, but that was quickly banished with a jealous wish that it could be me. That I could be the one to save her. That and the fact that Rage might very well be Harper's biological father leaves me with a heavy ball of anxiety deep in the pit of my stomach.

"Hey. You doing okay?" Lucas passes me a coffee.

I left to use the restroom half an hour ago, but right now, in the empty waiting room, I'm struggling to go back in.

I drag my hand over my face.

153

"You're worried what'll happen if he's the dad, huh?"

I stare at him; how does he always do that? Know my concerns.

I swallow past the lump of emotion clogged in my throat. "Yeah."

"Don't be," he simply says, and that angers me.

"Don't be," I mimic his words sarcastically. "Don't be? He might be her fucking father, Lucas. Then, Tia has everything she ever wanted!" I jump to my feet, ignoring the slosh of burning coffee on my hand. "Why the fuck would she need us?" I scoff at his ignorance. "They can be the perfect fucking family. She won't need us, Lucas." My lip quivers, and my heart freefalls. "I know she won't," I whisper.

"You're so damn wrong, Cole. She'll always need us."

I stare at him like he's an idiot.

"She's pregnant."

I startle. "What?"

"Pregnant." He holds up his phone. "Bloods just came back."

"Pregnant?" I repeat.

"Yes. She's expecting a baby. Our baby."

My breath catches in my throat, elation cursing through me. "Oh, thank fuck." I pace the room. "Jesus. Thank fuck."

I turn on my heel to face him again, because if her bloods are back, that means . . . "Is he a match?"

"He is."

"Is he . . ." I selfishly can't bring myself to say it, to

154

say the words when I so desperately started out hoping one day, I'd get the opportunity to be her dad.

"The doctor's in there now."

"Answer the fucking question, Lucas."

"He is."

I sink into the chair, my mind racing with so many feelings: guilt, envy, excitement, relief.

Devotion.

RAGE

I pace back and forth.

"Jace, sit down." Thalia's delicate voice can barely be heard among the beeping of the machines.

"How fucking long does it take to check?"

I turn around and find Harper's face. The pain of seeing her like this makes my gut clench in fear and anger. No child should ever be like this. Ever.

"Do you . . ." I clear my throat and try again. "Do you think she looks like me?" I ask Thalia with hope.

Her face softens, and I watch as she swallows. "When she was a toddler, I used to look at her and think she looked like you." She shakes her head as though bemused with herself. "I think I wished it more than I thought it. I wished it. Really wished it." Her eyes are brimming with tears.

Footsteps make my pulse race, and when the doctor walks in, I feel like he's stolen the air from my lungs.

"We have good news. You're a positive match for

Harper's blood type." I stare at him because I already fucking told him I was. "And you're also a positive match as her biological father."

The room spins.

Thalia chokes, and before I know what's happening, I'm lifting her out of her chair and into my arms. Our sobs combine. The wail that she releases is like nothing I've ever heard before, and I hold her tighter.

A cry of love, heartbreak, and relief.

CHAPTER

TWENTY

T ia

I'm still in shock from the DNA results, but I couldn't help the feeling of guilt when we told Lucas and Cole.

They both have visibly taken a step back, and I hate the thought. Cole has gone home to fetch us a change of clothes, and Lucas has gone to the police station to try and figure out what's happening with the Lancasters, but right now, I don't care. I just want my little girl to pull through.

"We can be a family, Thalia. A real fucking family." Hope spills from Jace as he stares at me from across the bed.

"We are a family."

He shakes his head. "No. Me, you, and Harper. Just like we planned. We can do this, baby. We finally have everything we ever wanted."

Ice fills my veins; he wants us to be a family. Without Cole and Lucas?

"I love them."

Jace's face turns red, and his jaw clenches tight. "We can have everything we ever dreamed of!" His voice booms, making me flinch, and he pushes back from the chair to stand. Back to pacing the room, he drags a hand over his head. "I could make you, Thalia." He turns his dark eyes to mine.

"Wha . . . what do you mean?" My heart races with the look of brutality in his gaze.

"She's my daughter, and you don't have custody. I could get custody."

I choke and gasp for breath at the same time. My face falls. "You'd take her from me?" Would he? Could he really do that to me?

He licks his lips, but his stare drills into me. He refuses to reply. "We could be a family," he repeats again, ignoring my question.

I swallow back the anger I feel toward him, worried I'm going to tip him over the edge.

"And I'd go back to hating you every day." My words come out low, but I know he heard them because he flinches.

A rustling noise makes my head snap in Harper's direction as her hand draws up to her face. A nurse rushes in and presses the button above her bed, and in the chaos, Harper's dazed eyes find mine.

"It's okay, peanut, Mommy's here."

"I want Cole too," she whimpers.

I kiss her hand, taking it in mine as the care team checks her over, my mind sending a silent thank you to whoever gave me back my little girl.

I only hope we can be the family I long for us to be.

JACE

I watch as my brothers fuss around my daughter and Thalia. I'm both annoyed and relieved that they're here.

It's clear that Harper loves them, and they're just as devoted to her. A sharp pain sears into my chest at the thought of what I've asked Thalia to do. Essentially break their hearts.

I was selfish. I was hoping for the dream we once had, but now, as Harper giggles at Cole's silly voices while he reads to her and the way Lucas watches them both with a soft smile, I realize we're already a family. As fucked up as it may appear to others, we're a family.

Thalia's eyes dart to mine, and I nod toward the door. She huffs but kisses Harper on her forehead and walks toward the door with me following behind.

As soon as the private waiting room door clicks shut behind me, I grab her by the arms and spin her to face me. Slamming her back against the wall, I rest my forehead on hers. "I'm sorry."

Thalia's eyes search mine. "You're right. We're a family. A fucked-up, brutal, devoted family." Her body sags in relief, and her fingers graze over my jaw. "I know it's not what we planned, Jace. But that dream was lost for me the day you left." I wince at her words, but she continues, "I had to make new dreams to keep away my nightmares, and those boys in there? They helped me do it."

I nod at her words. "I love you, Thalia."

"I love you too."

"I really need to fuck you." Her tongue flicks out over her bottom lip. "Jesus, so fucking bad." I groan.

She quickly works my belt and zipper down while I tug on her leggings and panties, kicking them to the side.

I hoist her up against the wall, and without any preparation, I spear her with my cock. My lips find her neck, and I tug on the flesh there. "Fuck, you feel good, baby."

I grind my hips when her fingernails claw into my neck.

"Jace, more."

"So." *Slam.* "Fucking." *Slam.* "Good."

Her pussy tightens around me, and her tits bounce against my chest. "Come inside me, Jace. Please come deep inside me."

"Fuuuck." We orgasm together, a maelstrom of messy make-up sex, and I couldn't be any fucking happier.

CHAPTER
TWENTY-ONE

Lucas

I end the call with the lawyer and turn toward Tia's hopeful eyes. Clearing my throat, I make sure Harper is asleep.

"Apparently, they were having an argument about you, and Harper was trying to run away to be with you." Her lip quivers, and she wrings her hands in her lap. Cole drapes his arm over her shoulders.

"My lawyer has moved forward with proceedings to place Harper in both yours and Rage's care. Now we have evidence she's biologically his, the case is even stronger."

I watch her closely as her throat works. "Will she have to go back to them?"

"No, baby girl. He's going to try and fix it so she can come home."

A lump catches in my throat at the meaning behind my words. She's coming home, and we're all going to be a family.

165

Finally.

"Jesus, that's amazing," Cole chokes out while clinging to Tia.

My gaze crosses over to Rage, who sits with his hand in Harper's. He's already studying me, and the thought what his plans might be unnerves me. Does he plan on ripping us apart before even giving us a chance?

He stills, then breathes out calculatingly slow. "That's great news, brother, we can be a family. Like we should be." He gives me a sharp nod, one that tells me a thousand things without uttering a single word.

Cole audibly exhales in relief before flinging himself around Tia, who is already sobbing in his arms.

I sit in stunned silence, a warmth spreading over me as I take in the room. All the people I ever cared about, all the people who mean something are in here.

Finally, we have our family.

TIA

Jace's legs bounce anxiously, and he chews his fingernail. I take his hand from his mouth and place it on my lap.

"You think she'll be okay staying with us? All of us?"

We turn toward the apartment building, and a wave of nausea hits me again. I put it down to nervous excitement, but it's been happening a lot lately.

"Are you okay?" Jace narrows his eyes at me before glancing back to the road.

"I'm fine, just nervous."

I watch him swallow before he gives me a tight smile. "Me too." He drags a hand through his hair. "Do you think we can tell her today? That I'm her dad, I mean." His voice is full of vulnerability, and my heart melts at the love I feel toward him.

"Of course."

His shoulders relax. "I just think we need to be a family now." I nod in agreement. "With Cole and Lucas too," he tacks on as though remembering them both. I smirk at his hiccup.

Fidgeting uncomfortably from side to side, I sigh and decide to tackle my next problem head-on. "I was thinking of staying in Cole's room tonight. With both of them."

Jace glances toward me when he pulls into the parking space. "Yeah. I think that's a good idea. They need you tonight."

I relax at his words. "Thank you for understanding."

"I don't care anymore, Thalia. I just want you and our little girl, and I want us to be happy." He stares at me with sincerity shining in his eyes. I trail my gaze down his face and along his tattooed neck. Wetness pools between my legs.

Jace breaks out into a huge smile. "You want my cock right now, don't you?"

My face heats, and when he brings his lips to mine, I melt into his kiss. His tongue wraps around mine, and I clench my thighs at the overwhelming urge to climb into his lap.

Jace pulls back to stare at me; his dark pupils sear into me with such possession and lust, it forces the air from my lungs.

"Fuck, you're beautiful. What I'd give to suck on your needy little clit right now. But, baby, our little girl is going to be here in"—he glances at the clock—"seven minutes." He re-adjusts his cock in his jeans.

The fact he knows down to the exact minute when

Harper is due makes me swoon for him even more than I am already.

I gift him with a playful smile. "You're right. Come on, let's go introduce our little girl to her dad."

Jace bites into his lip and his eyes fill with tears. "Okay." His voice trembles on a whisper.

Leaning forward, I press my lips to his. "I love you, and she'll love you too."

With that, we exit the car.

COLE

"What the fuck took you guys so long?" I spent the last twenty minutes pacing the room. The balloons are up, the fridge is stocked with all of Harper's favorite foods, and the surprise for Tia and Harper is all set.

"We got distracted." Tia blushes.

I raise a brow in response to her words before I scoff at her. "You suck his cock?"

Her eyes bug out. "No. We were . . ." She shuffles from foot to foot.

"I tongue fucked her mouth, and she made me squirt in my jeans." Rage breezes past her nonchalantly and heads toward his bedroom. I can't help but glance down at the obvious bulge in his jeans, and I lick my lips, imagining them together. Jesus, I have it bad.

Tia moves to wrap her arms around my neck and peppers kisses over my jaw, making my veins pump with heat. The thought of my girl being pregnant with my baby makes my cock twitch and causes her to chuckle.

She withdraws quickly, which is a good idea, as Harper is due here with Lucas at any minute.

"Everything ready?" Rage asks from behind me. I turn to see he's swapped out his cum-soaked jeans to gray joggers and a look that asks me if our plan is in place. I give him a subtle nod that has Tia shooting her eyes from me to him in question.

The door opens, and Tia startles before racing toward Harper, who has only just stepped foot inside the apartment. Tia drops to her knees and Harper hugs her. Tia picks her up in a tight embrace, and my palms twitch with need. All I want to do is rush toward them both and draw them close to me. Never let them go. They're ours now. Just as they always should have been.

Eventually, Harper slides down Tia, and her eyes take in the apartment. "I like it," she declares, making us all grin in response.

"Harper, we have a surprise for you." Rage steps forward.

"You do?"

"Yeah, follow us."

I hang back with Lucas and follow behind Tia and Harper as Rage leads them toward the spare room.

"Open it up." Jace motions with his hand for Harper to open the door while Tia stares at him in confusion.

Harper sucks in a shrieky breath. "It's amazing! I love it." She runs into the room and starts spinning around at all the pretty pink girly things.

When Rage suggested we create the perfect room for

Harper, Lucas and I put plans in place and have worked flat out to get it right for her homecoming.

"This is incredible, boys." Tia's eyes brim with tears.

I tuck a strand of hair behind her ear and gently kiss her lips. "It's okay, beauty. Please don't cry."

"I love you. You know that?"

I gift her with my megawatt smile. "I love you too."

TIA

The room is beyond beautiful. I trail my fingers over the pretty pink fabric of the canopy all the way to the animal teddies sitting at the foot of the bed. A true princess room.

My eyes latch on to the mural of a princess, the exact princess I've been drawing for the illustration contract. She stands with her hand outstretched, and in her palm is the key that Jace gave me. My breath stutters at the sentiment, and my legs wobble. She has the key to her heart, her home, and her family.

All in one, she has the key to everything she needs.

They found the missing piece to my drawing.

I close my eyes as emotion takes over me. Forcing out a deep breath, I gather myself to find Jace watching me closely. He steps forward, wrapping his arms around my waist, his face etched in concern. "Are you okay, baby?"

"I'm perfect. Everything is perfect."

His lip tugs up at the side, and he thumbs away a tear. "Was it the key?"

I nod, too overwhelmed to express my words.

"It was Lucas's idea."

I turn to face Lucas and detach myself from Jace. He's leaning against the wall, watching us all closely, always on the outskirts looking in. Glancing down at Harper to see her playing what appears to be tea parties with Cole, I move toward Lucas.

Giving him no warning, I grip his shirt buttons and pull him toward me. I take a hold of his neck and slam my lips against his. He barely opens his mouth, completely stunned at my desperate reaction to him.

Then, he appears to melt into the kiss; his muscles give way and his tongue sweeps in, making me whimper against him. I pull back when I feel the hardness between us.

"Jesus, Tia," he whispers, his pupils dilated.

"I wanted you to know how grateful I am and how much I love you."

His Adam's apple slowly slides up his throat. "I love you too." His words come out choked. "So fucking much," he whispers.

"Mommy, look, Cole is a princess."

I turn around to find Cole's cropped hair now covered in hair clips, wearing his signature huge smile. He looks utterly panty melting, playing there with my little girl on the floor.

Jace moves to be beside me, tilting his head low to

whisper in my ear, "Can we tell her now?" He fidgets from foot to foot, desperate to get it over with.

I nod, and he takes my hand in his. With Lucas right behind us, we kneel on the floor beside Cole and Harper.

Jace clears his throat. "Harper, we have something to tell you."

Her blue eyes look from me to Jace. "Are you getting married?"

Jace's eyebrows shoot up, whereas Cole glares in his direction, as though daring him to even utter those words.

"No, peanut, we're not getting married."

"Good, because I like you all, and I don't want you to have to choose."

My heart beats rapidly at my little girl, as though knowing I love them equally.

"I knew your mommy a long time ago." Jace's hand tightens on mine, as though he's struggling while searching for the right words. "We lost each other."

Harper flicks her head toward mine, sending her ponytail whipping into Cole's face. "You did?"

I smile softly at her. "I did."

"You found each other now, though." She glances down at our joined hands.

"Yeah, we did. When you were in the hospital, we found out that I'm your dad." He spits the words out quickly, and Harper's eyebrows narrow as she processes what he's trying to say.

"You're my dad?"

Jace exhales loudly, and his eyes fill with unshed

tears. "I am. But I only just found out," he tells her again, reiterating we only recently knew ourselves.

"That's cool." She shrugs as though it's nothing.

"Cool?" I reply, expecting a little more from her.

"As long as Cole and Lucas can be my dads too, because it's not nice to leave people out." She points at Jace with all seriousness, and he throws his head back on a relieved chuckle.

"Good one, Harps." Cole holds his fist out toward Harper, who bumps it with a satisfied grin.

"Lucas, you need to have your hair done too!" She points to one of the five small stools, and it's only then I realize the sweet gesture of there being five stools around the small table.

Lifting my head to stare up at Lucas, I can't help but laugh at the expression of horror on his face.

But when he drops into the stool beside her with a loud sigh, I think I fall in love with him a little bit more. Because who doesn't love a guy who's completely devoted?

TWENTY-TWO

C ole
Tia and Jace put Harper to bed about an hour ago. Lucas reassured Tia he had the room sensor working to alert us if she were to leave her room.

After numerous demonstrations, she finally relented to taking a bath while Rage and I sit with Lucas to discuss our next strategy.

Lucas withdraws a file from his locked drawer. I swear that guy has a vault of classified information in there on each of us.

"So, let me get this straight, you know someone inside who can finish him?" Rage asks, sitting forward.

"I do. But I was thinking, maybe you'd want to do it yourself?"

Rage's eyes light up, and a maniacal look that makes my heart pound and a wave of nervousness rush through me takes over his face.

"How?" he questions.

"He's due for release soon. The security firm I know, STORM Enterprises, can have him picked up the moment he steps foot out the prison."

"Do it," Rage's dark voice snaps back, leaving no doubt of his intentions. He's going to make him pay. "I want him."

Lucas grins back at him. "Good."

"What about the Lancasters?" I ask, because the way they've treated Tia and Harper cannot go unpunished. They tried to essentially steal a little girl. When all Tia needed was help and stability, they tried taking advantage of her circumstances, then made things as difficult as possible for them to be together.

"I've had their company liquidated." He glances at his watch. "Mr. Lancaster is currently being served papers for solicitation and fraud. They'll be penniless. I feel like I'm missing something about Mrs. Lancaster, though. But she'll suffer, nevertheless; she won't be able to survive without money." He smirks back at me, and I relax into the chair.

"Anything else we need to know?" I ask, growing angsty to be with our girl. After all, she promised us tonight.

"Yeah, actually, there is." Lucas drags a hand over his hair, messing it up in the process. "I found out some information about Tia's birth family."

"You did?" Rage asks, his face full of hope.

"She lost her parents in a car accident. She was born Anastasia Olska and has a sister named Jenny."

I take in Rage as he sits back in his chair, deep in shock. "A sister."

"Older sister. I managed to locate her too."

This grabs Rage's attention once again. "No shit! Where is she?"

Lucas rubs at his jaw, a telltale of his that lets me know he's unsure whether to say or not. "She's married to a Mafia don and goes by the name of Sky."

Rage stares in disbelief.

I can't help but choke. "Jesus."

"Right." Lucas nods.

My throat goes dry. "Do we tell her?"

Lucas taps his finger against his lip. "Not yet. Let me dig a little deeper."

"Is that it?" I ask, pushing up from my chair, eager to sink into my girl. My pregnant girl.

"That's it." Lucas nods, giving me the perfect opportunity to leave.

I STEP into my bedroom and instantly see the look of shock on Tia's face. She's sitting on the end of the bed in a towel with her phone in her hand. She's visibly shaking, and my temper flares at the thought that someone hurt her.

"What the hell happened?"

Her head snaps up in my direction, her face pale, and her eyes red. "That was the doctor. He said . . ." Her lip trembles. "He said I'm pregnant, Cole."

Fucking finally, I want to scream.

Instead, I smile broadly, and my chest puffs out in pride. "Pregnant, huh?"

I sit down on the floor between her legs. "That's incredible, beauty." I drag my tongue over my lips and stare at her stomach. I wonder when she'll start showing?

"Incredible?" She stares at me as though I'm mad.

"Beauty, you have everything you could ever need. Security . . ." I reach up and kiss her lips. "Love . . ." Another peck to her lips. "Devotion . . ." Our lips meet again. "You're about to give Harper a sibling, and I cannot wait to see her excited about it." Her lips tip up into a soft smile, and I know I have her.

Pressing my lips to hers again, I slip my tongue into her mouth on a low groan. "Fuck, I can't wait to see you full with my baby."

My cock leaks, and I slowly untie the top of the towel.

"Cole?" she pants in question.

"Shh, beauty. Let me make you feel good. Let me show you how much I love you and our baby."

I push her flat onto the bed and watch in awe as her breasts bounce. Her nipples look darker and larger than the last time I sucked them, I'm sure of it.

I spread her legs and quickly move to my feet to undress before dropping back to my knees. Using my thumbs, I separate her slick folds and inhale her scent before dragging my pierced tongue up from her hole to latch on to her clit. She bucks her hips up toward my face, and my cock jumps in response.

Tia's hand finds my head, and she holds me in place as I slowly eat at her greedy pussy. "More, please more." She thrusts harder against me, making me chuckle at how needy my girl is.

I surge two fingers into her, curling them toward the perfect spot, then withdraw them sopping with her cream before repeating the motion harder.

"Oh fuck, Cole."

"That's it, beauty, ride my face. Take what you want from me. Come on my face, Tia."

Tia thrashes on the bed, her tits bounce, and I long to mark them once more.

"More. More."

I withdraw my fingers as she begins to clench around me.

"Beg me for my cock, Tia."

Tia tilts her head up from the bed. "Please, I want your cock."

I stand, my cock dripping. "I want you to ride me, beauty. Ride me with my baby inside you." Her eyes fill with lust, and I know I have her. I know she's going to love being pregnant as much as I love the thought of it. Because our girl has three men to keep her satisfied, three men to be completely devoted.

I position myself with my head on the pillow, and Tia wastes no time in straddling me. "Lick your cum from my face, beauty."

My balls draw up when her wet tongue laps around my jaw and into my mouth, and when I position my cock at her hole, she drops her pussy down onto me, making my eyes roll to the back of my head with pleasure.

"Oh god, you feel so good."

"Stretching your pussy out for you, beauty."

I thrust my hips up hard into her, making her tits bounce.

"Yes. Yes. Please stretch me."

"Holy fuck, beauty."

One hand stays on my shoulder, digging her nails into my flesh, while the other starts playing with her nipples. The sight makes me want to come.

The bedroom door opens, and Lucas stands in the doorway. When he starts stripping, I can't help but think how far he's come from being the person who stayed in the background.

My hand finds Tia's stomach. "She's pregnant," I declare to Lucas, as though he doesn't already know.

He smirks as he moves around us calculatingly, and the knife in his hand glistens. "Mmm, perfect," he muses while taking in Tia's tits. "Suck on her nipples."

He stands beside the bed, jacking his cock with one hand, and the other is tightly wrapped around the knife.

"I'm on the pill," Tia pants in explanation.

My lips wrap around her nipple, flicking over the tight bud. A moan leaves her lips.

"I want you pregnant. It's good it didn't work, baby girl," he lies, and I can't help but love him for it.

Her eyebrows rise at his words.

"Daddy's girl, pregnant with his baby." He clucks,

and his cock drips pre-cum onto the floor, making me strain my muscles to ward off my own cum.

"Are you close?"

I nod back at him.

"I'm going to fuck her ass."

I nod again, because I can't find words, not when he's talking about fucking her together. Jesus, that's incredible.

"Stop fucking her a minute," Lucas snaps in annoyance.

Tia and I pant in unison as my thrusts come to a standstill on his command. Tia's panicked gaze meets mine. "It's okay, beauty. We'll make you feel good," I reassure her by stroking her clit lazily, causing her to mewl and relax in response.

Lucas slashes his hand with the knife, making us both glare in panic. We watch as he drips the blood over Tia's ass with lust-filled eyes. Then, he spits twice on Tia's asshole, and the moment he positions his cock at her hole, she jerks. Lucas's eyes close in euphoria as he slowly sinks inside her. I feel him fill her just beyond the tight barrier of her pussy, stretching her so we're positioned together. My cock involuntarily leaks, and I know I'm going to come quickly. "Brother." I panic, fisting the bed sheet in one hand.

"Shut the fuck up and take it. Take my cock in her ass." His filthy words don't help any.

"Please," Tia begs, her mouth slackened.

Lucas's muscles strain in his neck, and I know he's struggling to hold back too. "Suck her tits. Suck her tits and mark them everywhere," his ragged voice snipes out as his hips move, and his cock rubs against mine.

Tia holds out her tits one at a time as I suck them, tug them, and bite into them while she bounces up and down on my cock with Lucas's cock stuffed in her ass.

"Oh. Oh please."

"Take Daddy's cock, baby girl. Take it."

"Jesus, brother."

The room lights up from movement at the doorway, and when I find a wide-eyed Rage standing beside the bed, I can barely function enough to tell him, "She's pregnant." As though that's an explanation enough for us both to be fucking her.

His eyes flare with arousal, and he rips his shirt over his head, drops his joggers, and moves onto the bed.

"Jesus, Thalia. I can't wait to see your belly full, baby." Rage pumps his cock frantically. The veins on his neck protrude. "Such a dirty little whore, letting brothers knock her up."

My balls twitch on his words, and without needing instruction from Lucas, Rage moves closer toward Tia. "Suck." He holds his cock out for Tia, who bends her head willingly to accept him. Rage's tattooed hand tangles in her hair and holds her in place as we all fill her as one.

Love in brutal devotion.

TWENTY-THREE

S*ix weeks later...*

Tia

My eyes scan over the messy living area. Cole is on the floor with a pink duvet wrapped around him. Harper is nestled in Lucas's arms, wrapped in a blanket, and Jace has his arms banded around me with my back to his chest. His hands rest on the small baby bump now protruding from my body.

His soft lips nuzzle into my hair, and as always, goose bumps coat my skin.

"I can't wait for this little one to get here, baby. Then I can put a baby in there." His words make my thighs clench together. All three boys have been insatiable since finding out I'm pregnant.

Lucas scoffs from beside us. "I'm next."

I roll my eyes at their immature competitiveness. At my last scan, we discovered that I'm eighteen weeks pregnant, meaning that I conceived while I was just in a relationship with Cole.

"Do you want some more chips, beauty?" Cole tilts his head back to meet my gaze. I lean forward and press my lips to his.

"I'm good, thank you."

"I do!" Harper screeches and surges forward out of Lucas's arms.

Jace's arms tighten, bracketing me harder against him, as though protecting me and the baby from Harper's excitement. His action warms my heart with the fact he always looks out for us. Even though he was originally incredibly jealous of his brothers, he's now fully embraced our relationship and calls the baby his too.

"When I grow up, I'm gonna have three boyfriends too." Harper smiles as she shoves a hand full of chips into her mouth.

Jace tenses behind me. "Like f—"

"As long as you're happy, Harps," Cole cuts in before Jace can finish his sentence. I stifle a laugh, biting down on my lip.

"Apparently, twins run in my family, so you might get two for one." Lucas's eyes bore into mine before his eyes latch on to my stomach, as though imagining me pregnant with two babies. The stare is so intense, I squirm with excitement. The thought of gifting Lucas with a baby makes my clit throb.

"Harper, do you want Cole to read you a bedtime story?" Jace smiles sweetly at Harper as if sensing my need to be satiated.

Harper crosses her arms over her chest. "Nope, I want my dad to do it."

Cole turns his head over his shoulder. "Yeah, go on, Dad. Harper likes the thick story book too, don't you, Harps?" He smirks, making Jace release a growl.

"We'll take Tia to bed and make sure she's nice and warm." Lucas stands, brushing the chips from his joggers, a cunning smile playing on his handsome lips.

Jace grumbles behind me, and I can't help but smile as Cole takes my hand in his and pulls me to my feet, staring at me as if I'm a precious treasure.

Staring at me in complete love and brutal devotion.

CHAPTER
TWENTY-FOUR

Jace

I stare at the piece of shit that caused misery for our childhood. That ripped away the love of my life from me and then filled me with so much hate I became Rage.

I'm determined to drain as much pain as possible from him like he did to me by touching the only thing I had to love.

He snivels on the floor naked like a worthless sack of shit, trying his best to crawl toward the door with bloody drool dripping from his mouth. His hands give way in the pool of blood surrounding him.

I watched in delight as Cole pulled out his teeth, broke his hands and ankles with a hammer, and gave him a good beating. But I forced him to stop so he can feel the pain I want to inflict on him.

I hold out my hand for Lucas's knife, and he hands it to me. So much blood spilled due to this knife, yet so much pleasure too. It only seems right that it's this that finally ends this piece of shit. Finally ends her misery so we only have pleasure.

I yank his head back and slice down each side of his cheeks before dragging it lower toward his throat. His eyes flare. But if this sick fuck thinks I'd make it that easy on him, he's much more stupid than I thought.

"You remember the time you made me drink diesel fuel, Martin?"

His eyes widen in panic when Lucas steps forward with the canister, and I give him a firm nod to pour the contents over him.

He wretches and panics, choking on the fuel, and I delight in his terror. Excitement buzzes through my veins at making him pay for all the suffering he caused.

"Pin him down."

Cole steps forward on my command and holds his shoulders while Lucas steps around him. He tugs on some gloves that make me smile before he bends down to hold his ankles.

"You're a sick fuck, Martin," I spit at him in disgust. "You made me a little ragey."

Cole splutters in laughter. "Ragey, cagey."

I roll my eyes at him.

"Rage is going to cut off your cock, Martin."

His face crumbles. "Please no. Oh god, no." He sobs.

I shake my head. "I'm pretty sure you were told no so many times, and you ignored us," I mock while lowering myself to his cock. I can barely look at the wizened piece of shit. But with one swift action, I manage to slice the little fucker off.

Martin goes wild, thrashing about uncontrollably and howling in pain. I throw the fatty flesh onto his chest.

I drag the blade up his body, piercing him multiple times, careful not to make any of them deadly. Each puncture wound is precise to cause as much pain as possible.

"Help. Please help me." He tries to push against my brothers, whose gazes lock on to mine with matching maniacal smiles. They're enjoying this as much as me, and I couldn't be prouder.

He tries tugging, moving his arms, and in annoyance at his efforts, I snap at my brothers. "Snap his fucking arms too."

His eyes bulge at my words. Cole stands but holds one of Martin's forearms as he does. He steps onto Martin's shoulder, and the loud crack penetrates the air as he twists Martin's arm with brutal force, causing Martin to shriek with a gasping wail.

Then, Cole moves over to the other arm and repeats the action.

"You're going to burn in hell, Martin." I pull out the lighter from my back pocket. My dark eyes dilate as I stare at the flame, in awe of how such a small light is about to cause so much hurt yet so much pleasure.

"Wait, wait. I can tell you more . . ." he gargles.

I lift the flame and motion for Cole and Lucas to step back.

I barely hear his voice above his shrill screams. "Ahhh, please. I can tell you about the others!"

My face flares in delight as he becomes doused in a flaming ball of hell.

Finally, we're free.

Finally, I'm Jace.

LUCAS

We open the apartment door to find Tia pacing. She knew we were going to end him, and seeing her face drop in relief and fill with tears reinforces telling her was the right thing to do.

She throws her arms around Rage first, then she moves on to Cole, and finally me. She sniffs my neck and pulls back with a scrunched-up face. "Why do you guys smell of fire?"

Rage turns toward us with a maniacal grin. "Martin took a trip to hell."

Her eyes widen in shock before she clears her throat. "Well, can you guys go shower?"

"Are you going to join us?" Cole's eyebrows dance playfully, and she swats at his arm. Then Rage steps forward and scoops her up in his arms, walking toward his bedroom with Cole not far behind.

I stride toward the office and close the door, engaging the lock. My eyes latch on to the drawer.

The drawer that holds so many things yet to be discovered.

So many things still hidden . . .

TWENTY-FIVE

Six months later . . .

Jace

I stare down at Thalia with a fierce determination to plant my own seed deep inside her. I know Lucas is wanting to become a father next, but fuck that. I missed out on my girl's pregnancy and the first years of my little girl's life. If I want to be there from the start, I will be. Screw who has a biological kid and who doesn't.

I glance toward the baby monitor, knowing both Harper and Amelia are still sound asleep, at least for another hour, anyway. The moment Amelia stirs, so does Harper. It's both cute and annoying as fuck to have a full bed and being unable to touch Thalia how I want.

Amelia is six weeks old now. According to Thalia's doctor, she's good to have sex again. Not that I care if she's still bleeding, nor does Lucas—if he'd only admit the truth. We all know he's been desperate to fuck her now that he's got a taste for it.

I tug the sheet away from her body, exposing her smooth skin. She's lying across Lucas's chest with her ass in the air for the taking, but it's not her ass I want. Nope, it's her pussy.

Thalia stirs slightly, and Lucas on reflex tightens his hold around her. I drop my boxers to the floor and pump my cock in my fist, eager to have something else wrapped around it.

It's a wonder it hasn't fallen off with how many times I've jerked off imagining being back in her slick heat.

Since she gave birth, Cole made us promise not to have any sexual activity at all, to give her body time to recover. We couldn't even have a blowjob, no matter how much she was desperate for it.

I'm not sure who suffered the most through this dumb pact we made, us or her.

I climb onto the mattress behind her. With gentle kisses, I nuzzle into her neck and grind my cock into her ass.

"Mmm," she mumbles in her sleep.

My hand works down to her stomach, the incredible part of her body that carried our babies, and I couldn't love her anymore for it.

Thalia's hand finds my hair, the pinch in her embrace encouraging me on, so I trail my fingers down her stomach toward her panties.

She turns her head to look over her shoulder at me. "Jace. I'm still bleeding."

My eyebrows furrow because it's definitely six weeks. To the fucking day.

"Only a little," she reaffirms.

I nod and kiss her neck while I slip my palm past her waistband. "Do you think a little blood is going to keep me out of your pussy, Thalia?" I nip at her flesh, missing her taste on my tongue.

"Not a fucking chance."

I glide my fingers past her clit, desperate to feel the softness of her pussy. Her hole is slick and warm when I pump two fingers inside her. "Fuck, baby, are you turned on, or . . .?" I leave my question hanging, and she pushes her ass back at me in answer.

"So turned on."

"Fuck." I quickly slip her panties down her legs, ignoring the mess that women have to deal with from childbirth.

She spreads her legs wider over Lucas, allowing me to position myself further behind her.

"My cock is so fucking eager to fill you, baby," I groan as I rub the tip up and down her dripping pussy. "So eager to make you mine again."

I bite into her shoulder as I slip inside her pussy with a grunt.

"Ohhh," she moans as I fill her to the hilt with my cock.

"You okay, baby?"

"Yes. Please, I want you to move, Jace."

"Fuck." I pull back and thrust back inside, again and again, not caring if I wake Lucas in the process.

I notice his hand tighten on her shoulder. Then, he raises his head and glares at me. "You bastard, Jace," he spits out through gritted teeth. "I should cut off your balls."

I pull out and slam back in harder this time, forcing Thalia to cling onto him. I try to ignore the death threat he's glaring at me and instead choose to divert his attention.

"You're allowed to play with her tits now, Lucas. We know how much you've been wanting to taste them." His pupils dilate in response. I've watched Lucas's cock get hard each and every time Thalia has her tits out. How he's walked away to either compose himself or bash one out.

His gaze meets Thalia's, as though asking for consent, which is hideous, considering she'd give us anything anyhow.

She unclips her nursing top, exposing her bulging rack, and I have to freeze to stop myself from coming too soon. I bite the inside of my mouth.

Lucas's eyes widen, and Thalia gives him a quick nod of approval. He scrambles down the bed slightly to give himself access to her tit.

Her fingers thread in his hair, and I watch in awe as his lips meet her nipple. My cock twitches at the erotic sight.

Completely unlike when she feeds Amelia.

His eyes roll to the back of his head, and he closes his eyes in ecstasy. I never considered tasting Thalia's breastmilk before now, but watching my brother with her, taking what we helped create for our family, makes my cock spurt with excitement.

"Move, Jace. I need you to move."

My eyes don't leave her tits, they don't leave Lucas. I have a sudden need to make this moment between them everything.

"Baby, wrap your hand around his cock and stroke him. Make him come while he sucks on your tits."

Her lips part, and I know just the moment when her silky hand finds his cock, because his eyes shoot open, flooded with arousal, and he groans against her tit.

"Fuck, that's hot." I start moving my hips again, knowing I won't be able to stop myself from coming soon. "Fuck, Thalia. You're everything. You hear me?" I slam inside her. "Every fucking thing!" My balls tighten, and my body locks up tight as I flood her bare pussy with my cum. Her hand works quicker when my fingers press down on her clit, and she explodes, clinging to Lucas's head as his cum covers her fingers.

My chest heaves up and down when I notice movement at the bedroom door. Panic courses through me, automatically thinking it's Harper, even though I know we have an alarm on her bedroom door.

"You just couldn't fucking wait, could you?" Cole spits out while kicking off his sneakers and dropping his joggers, his cock already standing tall.

I chuckle as I flop down on the bed beside Thalia, taking great delight in the pink tinge coating my cock, thanks to her pussy.

Lucas detaches himself from Thalia's tit and drops

his head against the pillow. His tongue darts out to gather the droplet of milk on the corner of his mouth.

"Fuck me. Have you tasted her milk?" Cole drops his running shirt to the floor, his muscular body coated in sweat from his morning run. He always goes early before the little ones get up because he doesn't want to miss helping out.

"Yeah, and I'll be doing it all the time from now on." Lucas stares at him intensely, and it's times like this I want to take a step away from my brothers and let them figure their own shit out.

Thalia told me they haven't had sex with one another, but we both know it's only a matter of time until that happens.

"Jesus, beauty. Can I fuck you?" I roll my eyes, because of course, out of the three of us, he'd be the one to ask permission.

"I'm still bleeding a little."

Cole swallows hard, and his cock jumps. I swear Lucas has corrupted him.

"Yeah?" he all but chokes out. "Show me."

Thalia rolls onto her back and opens her legs. The sight of my cum mixed with hers makes my cock swell. Cole climbs between her legs and positions the head of his cock at her entrance.

"Such a good girl," Lucas coos as he moves to take her other nipple in his mouth.

"Leave some for the fucking baby!" I snap in annoyance, causing him to chuckle against her.

Taking my cock in hand, I work my palm up and down my cock to the motion of Cole fucking our girl.

Cole's thrusts become harder. "That's it." *Slam.* "Take my cock in your wet pussy." *Slam.* "Take us all." *Slam.*

I'm just about to come again at the live porn happening in front of me when a wail fills the room.

"Fuck no." I flop an arm over my face with a groan, knowing it's my turn to rise with the little ones.

Thalia turns her head toward me with a tight smile. "I'll just go wash my hands." I give her a quick peck on the lips, cursing as I drag myself out of our warm bed and away from Lucas's laugh.

I button Amelia's onesie back up after changing her diaper and giving her a pacifier to soothe her until Thalia can feed. I smile down at her with pride. She's perfect and content again for a short while.

I smooth over her soft, downy brown hair. Loving the feeling of her in my arms, I scoop her up and snuggle her against my chest.

"You forgot her blankie. She loves her blankie." Harper hands me the pink, fluffy rag with a giraffe on the end, and I chuckle at my little girl.

"You're the best big sister, Harps," I praise her, knowing how much she likes helping.

"I know." She grins back at me. Her two front teeth are missing, making her look cute as hell, and I take a mental snapshot of this moment, my two little girls together. We definitely need another boy to add to the mix. I smile to myself as I take hold of Harper's small hand.

"Dad? Why did Mrs. Lancaster come into school the other day but didn't come see me?" Her innocent question makes my blood still in my veins as I'm drawn to a halt by her words.

I glance down at my little girl holding my hand, trying to ignore the heavy pulsating thud of my heart. I clear my throat and try and keep my voice calm. "What day was it?"

"The other day."

"Which one?" Irritation bubbles inside me, but I tamper it down. Instead, I bend down to Harper so we're level with one another. "Try and remember Harper."

She presses a finger to her lip and taps it deep in thought. "It was the day I wore pigtails."

"Wednesday? Are you sure?" I distinctively remember doing her pigtails Wednesday, because for the first time ever, I did them right and got them level. Even Cole can't get them level.

Her bottom lip trembles, and she nods. "I know, because she doesn't like pigtails."

My jaw clenches, remembering how Mrs. Lancaster insisted on Harper looking a certain way, and she's right, she sure as hell wouldn't allow her to wear pigtails.

"Come on, Harps, let's get you both fed." We step out of her bedroom into the corridor just as Thalia and Lucas step out of ours. My eyes find Lucas's, and he must see something in my expression, because his eyes dart quickly around the room as though trying to figure out what's wrong.

I try to keep my voice low and my tone sweet, determined to not be the man I once was. To not be Rage again. "Harper, could you be a big girl and put the bread in the toaster?"

Harper gives me a shrug as I hand Amelia over to Thalia for her morning feed. "Sure, I'm gonna have two slices today." She holds up two fingers, and I give her a wide smile I don't feel.

I hear Thalia cooing at Amelia as Lucas and I turn and stride toward his office.

He spins on his heels as soon as the door closes. "What the hell happened?" His eyes search mine.

I can't help but pick up the paperweight on his desk and launch it at the wall. Rage bubbles inside me. "Fuck!" I scream out.

Lucas stares at me as though I'm deranged, his eyes moving back and forth over my face.

My chest heaves. "I want her dead, Lucas. Mrs. Lancaster. She's gone too fucking far. She's been in Harper's school."

Lucas physically jolts and stumbles on his words. "W-What?"

I nod. "She was at her school on Wednesday."

His glare turns menacing, and his hand twitches in his pocket. I can practically see him stroking his hand over his knife in the way that gives him comfort.

He drops his ass into his chair and scrapes his teeth on his lower lip as though deep in thought. All the while,

205

my temper is building, my muscles tightening, the rage bubbling.

"Suggestions?" I spit out, pissed at his silence when I need this shit resolved. Now.

"We reach out to Thalia's family."

My eyes widen. Is he serious?

We recently discovered Thalia had a sister she knew nothing about. Sky. Sky is married to an Irish Mafia don we know as Bren.

Lucas nods to himself, before going on to explain. "We reach out to Bren O'Connell and ask for their families' assistance."

"Assistance in what? I can fucking kill the bitch," I seethe.

Lucas shakes his head.

"Her husband was a senator, Jace. We can't just bump off spouses of senators without repercussions. Besides, how are we even going to get close enough to do it?"

I scoff at his words but stop myself from going further when the office door opens and Cole walks in looking freshly showered and practically bouncing happily with each step.

The door clicks shut, and his eyes dart from mine to Lucas's, his face falling with realization. He exhales heavily. "What did I miss?"

"We're about to go to war, brother." I smirk back at him.

THE END

EPILOGUE

Cole

I glance around the club again. I'm impressed with the layout; it's been well thought out with a classy vibe, not in the least bit sleazy like I expected, and the dancers don't look strung out, so that's a bonus for the paying customers. I take another swig of my beer. It feels like we've been here all night, when all I really want to do is be home with Tia and our girls.

Jace nudges me with his elbow, and when I turn my attention toward him, he nods at a guy with a toothpick hanging from his mouth. He's leaning against the wall, staring aimlessly into space, as though completely bored of the situation.

His hair is messy, and he wears a leather jacket and unlaced combat boots. As if sensing my gaze, his sharp blue eyes snap toward mine. A shudder washes over me, as though just from his stare alone I can see into his soul.

He has a sinister edge to him, that's for sure, into some fucked-up shit, yet he keeps it all tampered down.

I tilt my head to the side, surveying him as much as he is me. He reminds me of my brother before he found peace with his past. When he was Rage and not the Jace he is now. But I see the rage creeping back in. The anxiety to keep our family safe has him on edge, but I'm not prepared to let him give into his demon. So, here we are in a club owned by the O'Connell brothers. The Irish Mafia.

The guy I'm aware of is Finn O'Connell, one of Bren's younger brothers. He pushes off the wall and strides toward us with determination. His confident demeanor is impressive, considering he's about to sit down at a table with three equally deadly guys.

He spins a chair around, then he straddles it. "Talk."

I clear my throat to speak, but Lucas holds his hand up. "We want to speak to Bren."

The dude's lip slowly turns up at the side into a patronizing smile. "Sure you do." He raises his eyebrow mockingly.

I can feel the tension rolling off Jace. His body is coiled tight, and I can only hope he holds out long enough for us to get what we want. To get what we came for.

An alliance.

"He's here tonight," Lucas states, making the guy's eyes turn sharper, deadlier. He knows we've been watching, calculating the perfect time to approach him.

Jace's leg bounces beside me, and he stares at the table hard enough to drill holes through the damn thing.

But I'm proud of my brother for keeping it together, even though I can sense he's unraveling.

"If you want to walk out of here, you leave now." His voice is low and deadly, and his sharp glare penetrates into Lucas. But my brother is unperturbed. He's faced evil head-on, so this dude is a cakewalk for him.

"We have information."

The guy throws his head back on a condescending chuckle before he snaps his head back down with all signs of amusement wiped from his face. *Jesus, he's fucked up.*

"Don't you fucking all." He holds his hand up and snaps his fingers, and I watch on as what I can only describe as an army of men head toward us.

Panic bubbles inside me, and my heart races at the thought of us failing. "Wait. Fuck, just wait. It's about Jenny Olska." The guy doesn't so much as flinch with recognition at the use of her name. "Y-You know her as Sky," I stumble the words out, but it has the desired effect when he freezes and holds his hand in the air to stop his entourage.

His eyes snap toward mine. "What the fuck did you just say?" he asks, his voice somehow sounding even more sinister than before.

I swallow thickly but continue, relieved that I now at least have his attention. "Jenny, also known as Sky. We have information about her past." It's not a complete lie, but it is reason enough for us to be here and to grab both this dude and Bren's attention.

The guy trails his tongue slowly along his lip, as though deep in thought. Then he gives a firm nod of his head. "Okay. You have my attention. If your information is no good, then I'll fucking end you all for wasting my time." He smirks and stands, motioning for us to follow him with a tilt of his head.

We walk toward the metal staircase at the back of the club, the one with three armed guards at the bottom. I try to tamper down the feeling of trepidation as we follow this guy up the staircase, each step increasing my feeling of dread.

I can only fucking pray Bren O'Connell is a man who values family as much as we do.

At least then, we'll have a chance of getting out of here in one piece.

BREN

I stare down at my phone, trying to figure out what the hell just happened. Sky called me having some sort of bitch fit about Seb and Sammy emptying the contents of her toiletries into the bathtub. The little hellions switched the whirlpool jets on, and now our private bathroom resembles a foam party because they figured out how to put the damn speakers on too.

All this was happening while she was trying to feed Zachary, who is as clingy as a fucking koala. I don't so much as get a look in with Sky and her bulging rack. If I didn't enjoy getting her pregnant so much and get off on seeing her swell with what's mine, I'd tell her that's the last kid just so I can get her back to being just mine. Instead, I bite my fucking tongue and wait it out. Zachary is ten weeks now, so hopefully not too much longer. Isaac was way easier, that's for sure.

I scrub my hand over my head and sigh. How the fuck this is my fault when I'm in the office is beyond me, but she's like a wildcat when she gets stressed. So I told her I was sorry, and I'd send some guys over to sort the mess out, but when I suggested a nanny, she ended the damn call. I stare at the phone in shock.

Finn strolls through the door like he owns the room, and his presence alone makes my jaw clench because normally, following him is trouble.

My interest piques, and my shirt tightens across my back as my shoulders tense when three guys I've never seen before follow behind him.

"Sit," he barks out at them, barely sparing them a second glance.

The one in the suit takes a seat opposite me at my desk. He's well put together and looks like a business-man. The bigger-built one sits on the couch, and the one covered in tattoos glaring in my direction stands in the corner of the room, leaning against the wall. His jaw sharpens, and he pumps his hands into fists, making me aware he's gunning for a fight.

"I said sit!" Finn glares with fire burning from his eyes, making me wonder what the hell has been going off in my club. The tattooed guy glares back at him, equally enraged and not remotely fazed by Finn's outburst. Which is a rarity. My brother has a reputation giving him the moniker "Finn-finishing." His skills with a knife are next to none.

I don't know whether to be pissed at tattoo guy's nonchalance or applaud his gumption.

"Brother, please." The muscular one stares toward the tattooed guy. His eyes plead with him as though his life depends on it. I drag a finger over my lip and watch with intrigue as he pushes off the wall with a huff and plonks himself on the couch opposite, I guess . . . his brother?

They don't look alike, that's for sure.

Finn crosses his arms and leans against my desk, staring down at the suited one. "Apparently, they have information on Sky."

My spine snaps straight, and my hands ball into fists at the mere mention of my wife's name.

I grind my jaw. "Talk," I grit out, the anger evident in my tone.

"We need help with a situation," Muscled Guy starts talking. "Sky has a sister."

I try to fight the wince at the mention of Sky's sister. It's something I've failed to tell her, and I never intend on doing so either. Sky was separated from her younger sibling and sold to human traffickers. She has no recollection of her birth family, and I keep quiet with what little knowledge I do have. Afraid to hurt her further, I made the decision to not mention what I know at all. Which wasn't a fucking lot, only that she has a younger sister, and she went missing too. I assumed something bad must have happened to her, and therefore, I chose to protect my wife from suffering further.

"Her name is now Thalia," Suit adds on.

I nod in understanding. Clearly, it's someone they care about. Maybe they grew up together?

His eyes narrow on me, his voice turning menacing. "But judging by your face, you knew about her already."

213

Clearly, I'm shit at hiding my expressions.

I shrug arrogantly. "I was protecting my woman; she knows nothing about her. Sky has been through enough. I assumed her sibling passed away." I sit back in my chair and exhale loudly, feigning boredom.

This pisses off Tattooed Guy, because he jumps to his feet and throws himself across the desk toward me, but his brother holds him back with his arms wrapped around him tightly. Tattooed Guy's face is red, his veins protrude on his neck, and his eyes bulge in hate as he struggles in the embrace to get to me.

"You steroid-built motherfucker! Been through enough? What the fuck do you think my girl has been through, huh?"

I should correct him and tell him I've never touched a damn drug in my life, but something tells me he wouldn't listen right now, and I'd be wasting my breath.

"We want your fucking help. She's fucking family!" His words sear under my skin, and I feel a prickle of guilt.

He continues his tussle. "Have you got kids?"

Finn moves in a flash at the mention of our children. He whips out his knife and holds it against his throat, making both him and his brother freeze.

Suit is still seated, and he ignores the outburst. "We don't want any trouble." I scoff at his words. "Thalia and our girls are in danger." I sit forward in my seat with sudden interest.

He goes on, saying, "The ex-senator, Lancaster . . ." I chuckle mockingly at the name I recognize. ". . . him and his wife have an interest in Thalia." I swallow hard, unsure where this is going, but I'm acutely aware of what that scumbag has an interest in. Suit continues talking, "They're plotting something regarding—"

"My little girl!" Tattooed Guy screeches out, blood now dripping from where Finn holds the knife against his neck. And for the first time since setting eyes on them, I realize where this guy's anger is coming from. Someone is threatening his kid.

"Finn, back the fuck off!" I bark. He does so instantly but stands only a foot away from them.

"Sit." I nod toward the chair at the guy buzzing with rage.

He pushes off the muscle guy in a huff and flops down in the chair. His jaw clenches as he tries to restrain himself.

I pinch between my eyes, already pissed at being dragged into something I have no time nor business being involved in.

"Back the fuck up and start again. Who are you?" I pose the question toward the one who seems to have his shit together the best, even though he looks like a sinister version of my brother, Oscar.

"I'm Lucas. This is Jace." He throws his arm out toward Tattooed Guy. "And that's Cole." I nod at his words. "Thalia and Jace have a little girl, Harper. She was brought up by the Lancasters."

"Why?" Finn chimes in before Lucas can even finish the sentence.

"Because some sick fuck raped Thalia when she was a teenager, and they tried to adopt Harper against

215

Thalia's wishes." Jace glares in my direction, the hate behind the words aimed at me for insinuating Sky was the only one who had a troubled background.

"Jace and Thalia now have full custody over Harper. The Lancasters should be out of the picture, but Harper mentioned Mrs. Lancaster has been in her school. I checked it out." He grimaces before continuing, "They've been following Thalia and Harper."

Jace's head snaps toward him accusingly, his body coiled tight. It's obvious this information is new to him.

"I'll fucking kill them myself." I watch the dude unravel before me, his chest rising faster by the second.

I hold my hand up. "You do that, you're gonna get caught. You wanna be there for your girls, right?"

His venomous glare shoots toward me, and he gives me a firm but reluctant nod.

"What about you?" I gesture toward the one called Cole.

"I'll do it if I have to. We need to make it look like an accident, though. I have my girls waiting for me. I don't want to do time unless I have to."

"You married?" Finn raises an eyebrow at Cole.

Jace scoffs. "No, he's not fucking married. If anyone's going to marry her, it'll be me."

My mind takes a moment to go over what he just said.

"You both fuck her?" Finn questions before I can get the words out.

"The three of us, actually." Lucas's lip curls up at the side, a hint of pride behind his words.

Jesus fucking Christ, this girl has three men on the go. I blow out a heavy breath in shock. Holy shit, Sky's little sister has three men and . . . "How many kids?"

"Two . . . For now," Lucas tacks on at the end, and I don't miss the insinuation. Actually, I recognize it well.

I try to pull my mind away from their private lives and deal with the actual problem.

I clear my throat. "So, you want us to end the Lancasters?" I query. "Then we're done." I look at them pointedly.

"You don't want Sky to know her sister?" Cole asks, hurt mars his face. I chuckle at the thought of the big dude looking like someone kicked his puppy.

"She has all the family she needs." I stare back at him heartlessly.

"Right. So, you finish the Lancasters and we keep our mouth shut about her sister?" Jace reiterates my insinuation with a tic in his jaw, obviously pissed with my proposal.

"Exactly that." I tap on the desk, concluding this impromptu meeting is finished.

"You're a fucking dick, man," Cole spits out petulantly.

I gift him with a smug smile. "A huge fucking dick." I give my business card over to Lucas. "It has a copy of Oscar's, my brother, personal cell number on the back for you to use as a point of contact."

The three of them rise from their seats.

"Oscar will be in contact tomorrow," I speak to Lucas and ignore the death glares from the other two. He gives me a nod but nothing more, so I don't offer my hand for him to shake.

Cole stops as he's about to walk through the door. His eyes soften as he looks at me. "You know, our girls could use some cousins."

It's an olive branch, but being the bastard that I am, I refuse to deal with any more dramas. We've had enough of those in our family to last us a lifetime.

"Mine have enough cousins." My eyes drill coldly into his, and his shoulders sag on my words.

"Not every fucker is lucky enough to have a family; some of us make our own," Jace snipes back before turning and walking out the door with the men he calls brothers.

I sigh in relief when they leave, but a niggle of guilt tears through me at both their words and the image of another woman looking so similar to Sky and the fucking hell she must have endured.

I swipe the contents of my desk onto the floor in frustration with myself, letting out a roar in the process.

With a heaving chest, I snap my eyes up toward Finn. "Find out every fucking thing you can about them."

He gives me a sharp nod and takes out his phone.

I sit back down in my chair with a sense of unease, a sickening feeling of dread lining my stomach, knowing this isn't the end.

Knowing it's only the beginning.

NOTE TO READERS...

Please note this book is based after the Secrets and Lies Series has been completed. Including after CON'S Wedding Novella.

AFTERWORD

If you would like to read more about BREN and his story, a sample is available here...

BREN

ACKNOWLEDGMENTS

1 year on and eight books later!
Tee the lady that started it all for me.
Thank you, thank you, thank you!

I must start with where it all began, TL Swan. When I started reading your books, I never realized I was in a place I needed pulling out of. Your stories brought me back to myself.

With your constant support and the network created as 'Cygnet Inkers' I was able to create something I never realized was possible, I genuinely thought I'd had my day. You made me realize tomorrow is just the beginning.

To Kate, thank you for your dirty mind and
friendship. The perfect partner in crime.

Emma H, thank you for all your support.
Martina Dale, thank you for being there.
Thank you to Jenn and Tash for being so supportive.
Savannah, thank you for all your help and support.
Sadie thank you for your words of wisdom.
Elizabeth S, thank you for your steady stream of videos. I
love them, thank you!

Swan Squad

A special thank you to our girls;
Bren, Sharon H, Patricia, Caroline, Claire, Anita, Sue and
Mary-Anne who constantly support me.

Beta Readers

Thank you to my Beta Readers for all your help. Your
advice and support is much appreciated.
Libby, Jaclyn, Kate and Savannah.

ARC Team

To my ARC readers thank you.
I have such an incredible team, I couldn't do it without
you.
All your message, shares, graphics and reviews are
amazing, thank you.

To my world.

My boys, I'm incredibly proud of you both.
You can be anything as long as you're happy.

To my hubby, the J in my BJ.

Love you trillions!

About the Author

BJ Alpha lives in the UK with her hubby, two teenage sons and three fur babies.
She loves to write and read about hot, alpha males and feisty females.

Follow me on my social media pages:
Facebook: BJ Alpha
My readers group: BJ's Reckless Readers
Instagram: BJ Alpha

ALSO BY B J ALPHA

<u>Secrets and Lies Series</u>

CAL Book 1

CON Book 2

FINN Book 3

BREN Book 4

OSCAR Book 5

CON'S WEDDING NOVELLA

<u>Born Series</u>

Born Reckless

<u>The Brutal Duet</u>

Hidden In Brutal Devotion

(The Brutal Duet Book 1)

Printed in Great Britain
by Amazon